CROSSING
THE LINE

CROSSING THE LINE

GILLIAN PHILIP

BLOOMSBURY

LONDON · BERLIN · NEW YORK · SYDNEY

Bloomsbury Publishing, London, Berlin and New York

First published in Great Britain in 2009 by Bloomsbury Publishing Plc
36 Soho Square, London, W1D 3QY

A CIP catalogue record of this book is available from the British Library

ISBN 978 0 7475 9993 7

The paper this book is printed on is certified independently in
accordance with the rules of the FSC. It is ancient-forest friendly.
The printer holds chain of custody.

FSC
Mixed Sources
Product group from well-managed
forests and other controlled sources
Cert no. SGS - COC - 2061
www.fsc.org
© 1996 Forest Stewardship Council

Typeset by Dorchester Typesetting Group Ltd
Printed in Great Britain by Clays Ltd, St Ives Plc

5 7 9 10 8 6 4

www.bloomsbury.com

For Lucy and Jamie
and for Ian, of course

BACK WHEN

In this life you have to look after yourself. It's not that your parents don't want to take care of you; it's not that they don't have the best of intentions. It's just that parents have other things on their minds. They have things to do. They look away.

Like Dad looked away from the paddling pool.

I don't know how much of this is my own memory, and how much is what Dad told me later. Because he did tell me. He never let me forget it.

My sister Alexandra was strange and quiet from the day she was born, checking us out with her enormous dark eyes till she found she liked us enough to stay. The midwife said she was comparing the world to the way it was the last time around, and finding it slightly wanting. Mum liked this. Mum believed in reincarnation the way she believed in almost everything else, so maybe Allie really was a tsarina in a previous life. She certainly acted like one.

The first time I was admitted to her presence, I leaned on the chair arm and stared at her as Mum, Dad and a procession of friends and neighbours gurgled at the baby and ignored me altogether. Which was funny, because Allie was ignoring them entirely, too, her dark liquid eyes locked on me. If it's possible, given that her mouth was clamped round the woman's nipple, she was even ignoring Mum.

Not knowing what to do with my hands besides unscrewing the baby's head or trying to pull off its toes or something (I was only three and a half), I shifted from foot to foot and thought longingly of my electronic-sound Buzz Lightyear. I already felt inferior but Nan Lola took pity on me. She was a little out of the circle too, and as I glanced up, bored almost to infanticide, I caught her mischievous smile. Her hand covered mine and squeezed it, and her creased girlish face beamed down at me and only me. Then Nan Lola winked, as if to say *You're mine now, Nick.*

And I was.

Allie hardly ever cried. Not that she was one of those giggly happy babies; her silence was still and solemn and deadly calm. Apparently this is not an adorable trait in a baby, though I for one was pleased with it. I think Mum was unnerved by her ever gazing coolly into the middle distance and not looking terribly bothered.

So Allie was handed over to Dad, and they had their bottle feeds together. Very bonding, I'm sure, but it pushed me even further off the radar.

This is probably why I tried to kill her.

I remember that the day was hot, June-hot. Mum was holed up in her little understairs office in the house, on the phone to some magazine editor; Dad, of course, had gone for another beer. When Dad was sad he smelt of whisky, but that was usually in the evening. By midday he'd be only mildly gloomy, or maybe tired, and he smelt only of beer. I knew the difference very early.

That day I sat beside my little sister in the paddling pool, our bottoms cold in the freshly hosed water, our heads hot under our cotton legionnaire hats. She watched me, her pupils darker than ever in the shade of her hat brim but glittering with the sun bouncing off the pool. And I hated her as only a child can hate.

Several things riled me. Her unswerving gaze. Her silence. The fact she was only nine months old and she wasn't even fit to play with. And the reddening of her cheekbones, the concentration in her dark creased eyes, that meant she was about to poo in her swim nappy.

It offended me beyond belief. The shameless, remorseless nerve of her. I thought about grabbing the end of the hose out of the corner of the pool, where it was still churning out water, and skooshing it straight in her impassive face. That'd make her cry, all right.

But I didn't dare. Instead I made a face at her and shoved her hard, so hard that she toppled over backwards into the water.

I looked down at her, and she stared solemnly back. The rippling, sun-dazzled water made a sweet little round frame for her face and it was creeping up her cheeks and forehead and chin. She looked a bit astonished but not scared. I wondered whether to let her lie there and I wondered what would happen.

I knew I'd find out faster if I put my hand on her face and pushed her gently down. So that's what I did: I pressed on her nose with a forefinger and watched.

The water was trickling into her nostrils when I changed my mind. Reaching for her wrist, I tilted her back up on to her bottom. She sneezed out water, wobbled, got her balance back and smiled at me. It was a huge direct smile, just between us. I basked in it and smiled back, loving her for the first time.

Then she was snatched up and away from me. When I squinted into the sunlight I saw Dad, unsteady and panting for breath, Allie clutched against him, and he was staring down into my face, anguish all over his own. So I knew he'd seen me from the house.

At least, he'd seen me shove her in. Then he'd come running, but he hadn't seen me rescue her. So who did he think had pulled her upright? The pool fairies? Who would have saved her if I hadn't been there? Honestly.

'Never do that again,' he shouted. 'Never, never, never.'

You know, I think he was talking to himself.

I never did do it again. *He* did. It wasn't the last time he left her, just for a minute, just to get something out of the fridge. It wasn't that he loved Mr Carlsberg more than he loved Allie, of course he didn't. But each time he must have balanced the possibilities, and reckoned he had a moment to spare.

So occasionally I had to stop her climbing into a filing cabinet, or sticking her finger in a socket, or grabbing a pan off the stove. Mum was very busy, writing or broadcasting, and after all she knew Dad was keeping an eye on us. Besides, I loved my alien changeling now, fiercely, violently. There's a photo of me at five years old, the toddler Allie gripped in my arms, and I'm glaring defiance at the camera because she's *mine*. My dour eyes glower out from under straight jutting brows: menacing even at that age, I was.

When Nan Lola came to live with us, Mum thought I was upset. She couldn't have been more wrong: I was crying with sheer relief. I'd been terrified of starting school because it would mean leaving Allie to be supervised largely by Dad. Nan Lola understood this and she understood Dad, so for my sake she oversaw Allie like a benevolent hawk. She loved Allie, of course, but she guarded her principally for me. To make me happy, to make me feel secure. I was Nan Lola's one true love and

I knew that would never change.

But nobody is there for anybody all of the time. So the central fact of life is this: you have to look after yourself.

NOW

1

I knew that voice on the radio. Warm and folksy and caring. Sympathetic words of wisdom to get you through the day. That's what the slot's called: Words of Wisdom.

This was not a nightmare, unfortunately. I knew that because I'd just woken from one, and now I wished I was back in it. Rolling on to my stomach, I hauled my duvet over my head and crammed it against my ears. The voice was still an audible murmur, so I hummed till I thought it had stopped.

I surfaced just in time to hear a jaunty 'Goodbye, and good day!'

Good day? She'd just destroyed mine. If she hadn't tidied my pit yesterday and messed around with my radio, I might have lived in blissful ignorance till I got through the school gates. Come to think of it, maybe an hour's warning was just as well. I yanked the duvet down and spun the tuner back to its proper position, then turned up the volume so it would drown me out.

'Good day, Mother,' I moaned. 'You utter, utter cow.'

I didn't mean it. Much. At least, I wouldn't want her to hear it, since as far as I know she still has sensitivities. None of which, obviously, coincide with mine or Allie's, or she wouldn't do this to us.

Poor old Allie.

I'd have liked to spend ten happy minutes fantasising about wild sex with Orla Mahon, which took up a lot of my time lately. (Fantasising, that is, not actual wild sex.) But Mum had killed the mood, so I dragged myself out of the warm tangle of duvet into a cool August morning.

Barefoot, I padded through to Allie's room. Mum had hung one of her stupid crystals outside, so I used it to rap on the door, then waited for Allie's grunt, though I knew I could walk in with impunity. There was no way she'd be out of her bed. Indeed, in the dim light I could see only a misshapen heap of duvet and a splayed fan of impossible hair. Her radio was chuntering inoffensive eighties pop: Mum's local station again. I sat down on the edge of her bed and tousled the hair. 'Morning, Allie.'

Fingers appeared on the edge of the duvet and shoved it down, revealing her delicate face. Delicate but incredibly grumpy. Her eyes were sandy with sleep, what you could see of them through the strips of brown hair.

'Nick,' she said, 'you're sitting on Aidan.'

I sighed and shut my eyes. It was too early in the

morning for this. I'd had that disturbing nightmare and I was still sleepy. In fact I was drowsy enough to drop off right here and slump over sideways on to Allie's bed and start to snore . . .

'Get *off* him!' She was shoving and punching me, and her voice was turning shrill. 'Get off!'

OK, game over. I shouldn't have started it in the first place. Sighing, I righted myself and shuffled round to sit obediently on her other side. 'Better?'

She was still glowering at me. 'You'd better ask him.'

'Allie –'

'Forget it. Don't bug me in the morning. And don't bug Aidan.'

'OK.' I smiled at her. 'Sorry.' And I genuinely was.

Her dark eyebrows were still bunched in a resentful frown, but when I sorted out the blunt spikes of hair across her eyes, tucking them behind her ears, her features softened and I finally got a smile.

'You can feed me a grape while you're at it,' she said.

'Oh aye? What's wrong with Aidan?'

'Aidan,' she sniffed, 'doesn't do food.'

Everybody knew fourteen was way too old for Allie to have an imaginary friend. One of these days, one of these days very soon, I was going to have to have this conversation with my sister. For her own good, as well as for mine and the whole family's. But not right now. And not, at any point in the future, at half past seven in the morning. 'You're hell first thing, aren't you?'

'Only because my mother is a minion of Satan.' She wiggled her eyebrows.

'Allie,' I growled, then grinned. 'You heard it, then.'

'Oh God. Did I ever.' She pulled the duvet back up over her head. 'Nick,' came her muffled voice, 'I don't want to go to school today.'

'Tough,' I said. I tugged the duvet down from her face.

'We're not going. We talked about this already.' Back under the covers she went. 'You can't make us go.'

'Allie, you're beginning to sound like Gollum. *You can't make us, preciousss.*' I peeled back a corner of duvet to hiss it in her ear, and she squealed crossly.

'Get lost, Nick.'

'Allie, it's all right for Aidan. He can hardly get excluded, can he?'

'Yeah, and they won't exclude me either. Just you watch.'

'Allie,' I began, then stopped, too much of a coward to tell her off for being manipulative. My sister had Issues. Of course people didn't like to face up to her and tell her not to be so damn naughty. Anyway, it was everybody else who was uncomfortable with her Issues. Allie was perfectly fine with them.

Abruptly Allie flung off the duvet and sat up. Her wild hair fell across her face, so she pushed it back with one hand. First thing in the morning it was just like her: a mess. When she'd brushed it, it would hang thick and straight, a blunt wedge of hair that could swing forward to screen her eyes. Together with her sulky mouth, her angular brows and massive dark eyes, it made Allie look like a manga heroine, brave and adorable and jaggedly beautiful. She didn't look anything like me. I had shaved brown hair and straight jutting brows and a narrow mouth. And a hard jawline, and a nose that was slightly too big and once got broken. Rugged, Mum would say kindly. Thuggish, said almost everyone else.

Allie was staring at the opposite wall, wide-eyed and haunted. 'Today's the day.'

'Yes,' I told her gently.

She turned and gazed at Aidan.

No, no, no. She had me at it now. What I mean is, she turned and gazed at the place she imagined Aidan was.

'How d'you think he feels?' she snapped.

'Well, don't have a go at me,' I said. 'It's not my fault.'

'I know. OK. But how could Mum?'

'Yeah, yeah.' I agreed entirely. 'Bad timing.'

'Doesn't she even think?'

'Allie, I don't think it really occurs to her.'

'God.' She scowled. 'She must have changed the radio yesterday, it drives me mad when she does that. Came on ten minutes ago and there she was. I could've died.' Her almost-black eyes widened and she nipped her lip and glanced aside. 'Sorry.'

I sighed and rubbed her shoulder. 'I'll go and wake up Lola Nan.'

'She's awake,' said Allie. 'She's been awake for hours.

She was hoovering downstairs. She woke me up at four o'clock and I've hardly slept since.'

'Liar,' I told her. 'Get up. And you,' I added in Aidan's direction.

Just to humour her, of course.

Allie didn't learn to speak till she was nearly two, at which point she found Nan Lola an inconvenient arrangement of consonants. So she took a unilateral decision to turn it round, and Nan Lola was Lola Nan ever after.

Yawning, I shambled downstairs. I thought Lola Nan had stopped hoovering, but when I pushed open the lounge door she was still at it, only the Hoover wasn't switched on. Her head jerked up and she stared wildly at me, shoving the vacuum cleaner back and forth. Her bone-white hair stuck out all over, as if she'd plugged herself into the socket by mistake.

'Want a cup of tea, Lola Nan?' I said.

'I can't hear you!' she shouted.

'Cup of tea?' I shouted back. God, I'd make someone a great husband one day. I was that used to humouring crazy women.

'WHAT?' she yelled.

I caught the flailing plug and stuck it back in its socket. The Hoover roared and Lola Nan went back to her pointless work. Pointless, because she kept going over the same two square feet, ignoring the rest of the gritty carpet.

In the kitchen, Dad had his hands over his ears. His eyes were tight shut: against what, I don't know. Maybe just the light. He ran from everything: shadows, light, reality. I was not going to grow up like Dad, that was my big ambition. I wasn't going to spend my life running.

'She's off again,' moaned Dad. 'She's been at it since four!'

'Morning,' I said, switching on the kettle. Really? Four o'clock? That would explain the nightmare, which was something to do with trains. 'Heard you just now, Mum.'

She turned away from the sink and gave me a bashful look. Mum was still pretty, with her wide-spaced hazel eyes and her tumble of auburn hair that sometimes showed tell-tale grey at the roots. It was pulled back into a rough ponytail as usual. At her age I thought she should really get it cut, but short hair wouldn't go so well with the loose hippy chick blouses and the glittery swishing skirts.

Besides, her ponytail was an improvement on Dad's, which was that shade of ashy-blond that looks as if it's always verged on grey. I think ponytails look great on a twenty-year-old, or a girl. Not on a rather drawn, worn-looking guy with mystical tattoos on his wrists that I'm sure he regretted. He regretted a lot, my dad.

'Words of Wisdom? You listened to me?' Mum's cheekbones pinked as a smile twitched her mouth. 'Oh, did you like it, Nick?'

'Yeah,' I lied. 'You were great, Mum.'

'Oh, thanks, love!' The smile broke open and made huge dimples in her cheeks.

Well. She's my mother. I'm not a bad person. At least, I'm not as bad as I used to be, but I'm still a great liar.

I'm never sure if Mum believes in God or Buddha or the fairies, but I suspect it's a peach-fuzz combination of everything. Her favourite song is 'Imagine', so she has a pan-pipes version to introduce the Words of Wisdom slot. Mum just wants everyone to be nice to each other. I'm not sure if she knows herself what she believes in, but neither does her target audience, and they don't care. She's very popular. She writes poems for the local paper and short syndicated articles for magazines, down-to-earth homilies that make you wince. I can't bear to read her stuff and when she asks for my opinion, I bluff. Just grunt on a positive-sounding note. You can get away with that when you're seventeen. Monosyllabic grunting is expected of you. It's especially expected of me.

The hoovering had stopped at last so I took Lola Nan her tea, but I didn't linger. She was sitting in her thread-bare wing-back chair, smiling at the corner of the room and nodding. Her right hand was patting the chair arm as usual – well, not quite patting it, but stopping about an inch above it, as if bouncing off an invisible cushion. Lola Nan's mannerisms mostly didn't bother me, but this one was really irritating, and I was tempted to take her hand and shove it aside to put the cup down on the chair arm. She must have sensed it, because she focused on me and growled like a bear.

Sighing, I squeezed round to the other side and put the cup on the chair's left arm. She probably wouldn't spill it so I left her to it.

Back in the kitchen Dad was glancing nervously at the ceiling, roughly where Allie's room might be if it was ten feet further south. For a bloke, Dad didn't have a lot of spatial awareness. 'Where's Allie?' His spoon hovered in mid-air.

'She's just coming,' I said.

'She's a bit late.' His spoonful of home-made organic muesli vibrated slightly, and milk dribbled on to his beaded placemat.

'It's the anniversary,' I said.

Mum's shoulders stiffened and she gave a little gasp, but she didn't turn round.

'Oh. Is it?' Dad blinked. He was trying his best to focus.

My dad has only one problem with alcohol: he doesn't find it a problem. He tolerates it just fine and he's never drunk but he always goes to bed looking vaguely dazed, and wakes up much the same way. When the shadows in his mind close in, though, and he flounders in self-pity and black misery, the only thing to do is leave the house.

Mum says he finds it hard to cope with Lola Nan, but I know he finds it hard to cope with life: he doesn't have the resources. He's underfunded in the defence department. Dad is a right one for getting into squabbles he can't win, then having to capitulate because he can't see it through. He always leaves it just too late to salvage his self-respect, too, just when the contempt of some traffic warden or neighbour or council bureaucrat becomes palpable. I'd seen my dad buckle and retreat and back off so many times, his pride pulled from under him like a rug, I could hardly bear to watch any more.

'The anniversary,' he said dully. 'Oh.'

Mum rubbed her temples with her thumb and finger. 'Oh Lord,' she said to the kitchen window. 'I hadn't . . . that hadn't . . .'

Occurred to you, I thought. Yeah. Quite.

'You've seen Allie this morning?' You wouldn't believe the aggression Dad put into that. 'Is she all right?'

I didn't answer, just poured milk on to my Frosties and pretended I couldn't feel his glare. I was the one person Dad could stand up to. Go ahead, I thought, if it makes you feel tougher. The best thing was to ignore him, since I knew he'd like to hit me but he'd never dare. Not after that first time.

Feeling the hostility, Mum sat down, over-brisk and bright, and clasped her hands. For a hideous moment I thought she'd ask us to say grace, but she unclasped them again and folded them round her mug of nettle-flavoured swamp water instead. 'A year,' she said, in her steady, professionally compassionate voice. 'A whole year. Perhaps we need to move on with our lives.'

'Some of us won't,' I muttered.

'Oh, Nick! Kevin Naughton was very young. And he

must have been very unhappy.'

Sometimes my mother's so generous and understanding I could slap her. Kev Naughton wasn't any younger than me, I thought, and I didn't do anything like that.

But I might have. That's the thing.

Mum was pouring herbal pee into Dad's mug and the flow juddered a bit. That's how I knew her hand was shaking. She said, 'Shh. Allie's going to be down in a minute.'

Adults are funny that way. Thinking a thing can't hurt you, just so long as they make a huge effort not to mention it.

It was like every other morning. I took Lola Nan some toast and Marmite, and made an effort to talk for a bit, and she yelled at me. Nothing specific, just a yell, but I left, and she ate the toast. Allie appeared, stopped dead and stared accusingly at the table, then ostentatiously pulled up a chair for Aidan. When Mum put on her happy face and offered to set him a place, Allie reminded her, in a tone of extreme patience, that Aidan Didn't Do Food. Dad looked troubled, Mum looked brisk and positive, and I ate my breakfast as fast as I could and got out of there.

Sometimes I liked Lola Nan's company best.

Before school I had my little ritual, same as ever. Pulling out the drawer at the bottom of my wardrobe, I pushed aside winter clothes and tugged out the narrow package wrapped in newspaper. I kept it sharp, for old time's sake, and even through several layers of *Daily*

Record I could feel the edge of it. If I pressed the tip, it could almost prick blood from my finger.

A blade is a beautiful thing. I'm not saying that to sound macho, it just is. It doesn't sparkle like sequins on a flouncy skirt. It doesn't have the glitterball dazzle of one of Mum's crystals against a sunny window. The gleam of a blade is smooth and flat and unbroken, shining steel, an understated glow. This knife felt light and flexible and true, and there was something reassuring about it.

So I was reassured. I did not want to unwrap it and take it with me. I never wanted to do that again but I always needed to know it was there. It was my totem, my charm. Pushing it gently to the back of the drawer, I laid the jumpers over it and shoved the drawer shut. Then I yelled for Allie, but she yelled back that she didn't need my company, she had Aidan.

And so I walked to school alone.

2

Allie was a cunning little witch. Aidan indeed. The reason she didn't need my company was that she really wasn't going to school. Unfortunately I'd sat through double English, a free period, the mid-morning break, several half-heard taunts about my mother's radio slot and double Biology before I realised.

Allie's Chemistry coincided with my Biology . . . (No, that's Orla Mahon . . .)

What I mean is, Allie's classes in the science block coincided with mine, so as usual I kept a sharp eye out for her as the corridors swelled with lunch-break crowds. Dodging the trouble spots and avoiding eye contact with the baby-faced dealers – I swear, they get younger every year – I hovered in the corridor that smelt of sweat and polish, sweltering in the sun that glared through the floor-to-ceiling glass. Somebody should have shot that architect and I wish it could have been me. My armpits were damp, my mood darkening; the skin of my face was corrugating into a scowl. Every one of Allie's class passed me, most of them giving me a wide berth, but Allie wasn't among them.

Allie, I thought, I'll kill you if you've . . .

And then I spotted Orla Mahon, lounging in the L-shaped bit of the corridor beside a half-dead pot plant, her loyal posse around her.

I glowered at a spot in the middle distance, as if I was still looking for my sister, but my gaze slewed helplessly to the left. Orla, Orla, Orla. Beautiful, big-breasted Orla, Clyde-built, made for wallowing, made for a long leisurely voyage. Her straight dark hair fell over one of her smudged eyes, the foremost hank of it dyed an improbable platinum blonde. I wondered if the nose ring had hurt going in, and I wondered if I could use that as a conversational starting gambit. I wanted to eat her sullen glossy lips. I wanted to eat her.

She felt me watching and glanced up, contemptuous. She said not a word, but by some kind of osmosis the posse too realised I was there, and they turned as one.

'I'm looking for Allie,' I snapped.

Orla looked at the girl on her left, then at the one on her right. Then she looked at me, upper lip curling. Her jaw moved around her chewing gum.

'Sheesh,' she said. All the boredom and apathy in the world went into that one syllable. 'Any Words of Wisdom for us, Nicholas?'

'Eff off,' I said. Except I didn't say 'eff', and what I did say I didn't mean.

One of the posse giggled, so I glared at her and she shut up. But I could feel Orla's stare, so I turned to her again. 'You seen my sister or not?'

I only asked for her help because I was desperate. Actually that isn't strictly true: I asked because I wanted to go on talking to Orla, even in these circumstances. But she didn't say another word. Her pewter irises glittered, outlined in that ugly black eyeliner. God, she was intimidating. God, she was beautiful.

Under the implacable hostility of five girls, I looked away and tugged my collar. Then I snatched my hand away, annoyed at myself. And that's probably one reason I got so furious when Shuggie emerged from the Chemistry lab, last as usual, and no Allie in tow. I stormed up and collared him, and he eyed me nervously through his thick geeky glasses. I gave him my best intimidating glower.

'Don't look at me like that,' he said. 'If you can't control her how am I supposed to?'

Sighing, I let go of him. 'She wasn't in class then?'

For answer Shuggie just rolled his magnified eyes, as if it was the stupidest question he'd ever heard. Which it probably was.

'I thought I told you to keep an eye on her?'

'How do I do that if she isn't there? She never showed

up. You're her brother.'

'Listen, you little dirtball, you were supposed to come and get me if this happened.'

'Look, Nick, you don't scare me.'

'Oh, really?' I got hold of his collar again and twisted.

He tugged himself away. 'Really. You're not a thug, Nicholas; you're an utterly unconvincing excuse for a thug.'

I stared at him. Beaten as usual by the little tick. 'Nevertheless, Shugs, there are days when I could happily kick you to death.'

'I'm sure. Let's move along now. People are staring.'

I swear, there were times I didn't know how Shuggie had survived two school years. I didn't worry for him, though. If he wasn't dead by now, he'd probably make it through. He certainly couldn't get any more annoying.

He walked alongside me as I turned and strode back down the corridor, which was embarrassing in itself, but I knew better than to try and shake him off. It would only make him stick closer. Shuggie seemed to think I was some kind of unpaid bodyguard.

'I really fancy your sister.'

The geeky little git. The nerve of him. I found there were no words for my disbelief, so I just walked faster.

'Course, she's so hung up on that Aidan, I haven't got a chance at the moment.'

'Shuggie, you haven't got a chance ever, in the entire future of the world.' I came to a dead halt outside the canteen and eyed him malevolently. 'Do not encourage her, right? Do not ever encourage her about bloody Aidan.'

'It's not my fault. You're her brother.'

'Like I could forget.' I peered through the lunch crowds, hoping she'd be among them, but hope didn't make her materialise.

'You're putting off the inevitable,' said Shuggie, dumping a yoghurt and a fruit juice on my tray.

I dumped them right back off. 'Shut up.'

'Where do you want to sit?' He picked up his own tray.

'Miles away from you.' I scowled at the dinner lady, who had just managed to flip a noodle against my sweat-shirt, where it stuck like a tapeworm. She was always throwing food at me. I think it was deliberate. 'Shuggie, go away.'

He shrugged. 'Who else are you planning to sit with?'

'Nobody,' I gritted. 'Nobody. I mean, that was the *plan*.'

He was Allie's age, for God's sake. Bad enough that he was a speccy little nobody, but the fact he was in my sister's year only made this more humiliating. They used to be in and out of each other's houses all the time when they were at primary school, and right after they went to Craigmyle High. Of course, that was before she decided to be best friends with some boy who didn't exist. Shuggie could hardly compete with the mythical Aidan, but I didn't see why he had to stalk me instead.

He was hovering now, trying to edge into the seat

beside me. The little tosser had the antennae of a hippopotamus. Around me other kids, depending on their personality, were either talking louder and pretending they hadn't seen me, or finishing their lunch in record time and buggering nervously off. I think my force field of disapproval might have scared off even Shuggie, but just then someone grabbed his shoulder and shoved him out of the way.

'Eff off, Middleton,' said Shuggie's usurper.

Oh, shit. Without glancing up I reached back, gripped Shuggie's arm and wrestled him into the place beside me. 'You eff off, Sunil.'

Shuggie was an aggravation, but he was my aggravation, and I wasn't about to let him be shoved around by the likes of Sunil.

'What's your problem, Nick?' snapped Sunil.

'I haven't got a problem,' I said, 'these days.'

He leaned down slightly, so Shuggie couldn't overhear. 'Look, I just thought we could . . .'

'What?' I gave him my foulest Tarantino glare.

'I thought I could sit here, that's all.' He was getting the message at last, tensing with hostility.

'So you can take the piss out of me with your mates? Forget it.'

'Aye, fine. If you'd rather hang out with Stephen Hawking Junior.' Sunil gave a short laugh and effed off.

I sat in silence, making myself eat rubber hamburger though my appetite was gone. Shuggie, catching the mood for once, stayed quiet. There was a chance Sunil was genuinely trying to be friendly. It was possible he'd been trying to make it up with me. I wasn't about to take the chance, though, seeing as the last time I saw him up close, it was through a film of blood and his boot was in my face.

I could feel a stare burning between my shoulder blades, so I turned. Orla and her gang were watching me with pure loathing, and Gina was murmuring in Orla's ear and giggling. I was about to flash her the finger when I remembered how God-awful yesterday lunchtime had been. Same as every lunchtime, of course: Allie, sitting beside a vacant chair, resting her chin on her hand and smiling at thin air. Spluttering giggles from some kids, embarrassed silence from others, meaningful murmurs between teachers. Sneers and pitying glances thrown in my direction as well as Allie's. Orla's gang sniggering. And Orla herself, face darkening with disapproval, finally getting to her feet and swanning disdainfully out, her gang in tow.

I was mortified, and furious with the lot of them. Allie was a bit eccentric, that was all. Kind of odd. They had no right to laugh at her.

But I was angriest with Allie. How could she do this to herself? *How could she do it to me?*

Thinking that way, remembering the horrors of yesterday, I was glad she'd skipped school today. I wished she'd stay away. For good.

Guilt kicked in like a Timberland boot.

'I'll have to go and look for her.' I rubbed my hand across my eyes.

'Yes,' said Shuggie, shovelling yoghurt into his face.

I checked my watch. 'I better go now.'

'I think you should have gone five minutes ago. Don't you?'

He was right, of course. I'd only been putting off the evil moment because I didn't want trouble and I didn't want to be responsible for my mad sister. But I couldn't put it off any longer, so I slunk out of the canteen and out of the grounds, unnoticed, wounded and feeling hard done by. Everybody had it in for me. Orla. The posse. Allie, for doing this to me. Even Shuggie, that itching louse on the bum of the school population. Sometimes I felt like the lowest form of school life. To think I used to be one of its alpha males.

I hunted all over town for Allie, and that wasn't easy. She didn't have favourite shops so I had to check everywhere and by the time I'd done one side of the High Street I reckon the security staff were phoning ahead to each other. *Shaven-headed thug coming your way, Darren. Scar on his right eyebrow. Broken nose. Lock up your CDs.*

Jeez. I must have been a gift to any genuine shoplifters that day, because nobody was watching anyone else.

Including my sister. I caught up with her in Drugstore Cowboy, shoving a bottle of shampoo up her sweatshirt.

'Put it back,' I growled out of the corner of my mouth.

She sighed dramatically and let the bottle fall back into her hand. Nestling it in her palm, she studied the ingredients. 'Go away, Nick.'

I stood right beside her, examining a display of conditioner. 'No.'

'Go *away*.'

'Allie, grow up.'

'No.' She made to stick the shampoo back up her sweatshirt so I grabbed it, prised her fingers off and dumped it violently back on the rack.

'And the rest,' I said.

'The what?' She blinked.

'The rest. Don't make me frisk you, Allie. Just don't.'

Her hand wandered towards her pocket, but without much enthusiasm, and losing my temper I pulled her wrist aside, shoved my own hand in and found three lip-salves. I yanked them out as she winced in exaggerated pain. 'Where do these go?' I could feel the beginnings of panic. I didn't want this. I didn't want trouble.

There was a presence behind us, a big, threatening, muscular presence. Bigger than me even. I turned my head.

'Is he bothering you, love?' The security man was talking to Allie, but his eyes were on me. I snapped my head back round to glower at the shampoo. I was going to kill her. Kill her.

Sliding a bottle of nail varnish remover elegantly from

pocket to shelf, Allie turned and gave the brute a dazzling smile. Her cheeks dimpled and her huge eyes lit up and her spikes of hair fell endearingly across both eyes.

'It's all right, Richie,' she said. 'Really. I can deal with him.'

Richie. *Richie?* The little criminal was on first-name terms with the security staff.

'I don't know about that, love.' The man's eyes slid from me to Allie, softening as they did so, then back to me, hard as nails again. He was making some point about the height difference and picking-on-someone-your-own-size, and I didn't bother arguing. Waste of effort, and anyway I couldn't betray her, tempting as it was. Sullenly I kicked a heel against the display stand, doing my best to outstare him.

'Honest. I'm fine. I can handle *him*.' Like I was some Neanderthal with gristle for brains. 'Don't worry.'

'If you're sure, love.' He tightened his biceps. Tosser.

Allie touched his arm, very lightly. 'Thanks,' she said. Manipulative little *witch*.

He gave us his undivided attention after that, and Allie turned on her heel, gave Richie another sweet smile, and left the shop. For pride's sake I hovered, scowling at him, for a few seconds more, then sauntered after her. Once out of the shop, I bolted.

As soon as I caught her up I grabbed her arm hard and dragged her along the street. I must have been hurting her but I couldn't help myself, and she didn't let on. I didn't speak to her again till we were a hundred metres down the High Street.

'Don't do that to me.' I felt like crying, which was humiliating and made me even angrier. 'Just don't.'

She shrugged. 'What was I supposed to do? Tell him you *were* bothering me?'

'You got me in trouble. You could've got me in a lot worse.'

'Quite. I could've got you in a lot worse. Stop moaning.' She smiled at me so unexpectedly, it took the wind out of my sails and I stood in silence, nonplussed.

'Did Aidan put you up to that?' I asked. I hoped things hadn't taken another turn for the worse with Allie. I hoped she wasn't really going mad.

'Course he didn't. I only did it to annoy him. Sometimes he gets up my nose, Nick.' Allie wrinkled it for proof. 'He's so self-righteous.'

I had to pause for breath, but I couldn't help asking, 'Does he mind you talking like that about him?'

'Not here, is he? He stormed off when I took the shampoo. I was fed up of him.'

'Allie,' I said, as gently as I could. 'If you're fed up, get rid of him. You can just get rid of him, you know.'

She stared at me, like it was me that was mad. It was a look that made me shiver. Then she shook her head slowly.

'Get rid of him? Of course I can't get rid of him. What d'you think, I can just tell him to go away? He cares about me. And besides,' she added solemnly, 'it isn't finished yet.'

Whatever she meant by that. 'Who says?'

'Aidan does.'

I swallowed over the hard constriction of my throat. Sometimes Allie terrified me.

And sometimes Aidan did.

I shook my head. 'Come on then.'

'Come on where?'

I pointed at my watch. 'Lunchtime's over. I hope you ate while you were thieving, because you haven't got time now.'

'I've got all the time in the world. I can't go back till I find Aidan.'

I grabbed her wrist. 'Aidan can go play with the trains. You're coming back with me.'

Allie didn't resist and she didn't pull away. She just turned quietly, her eyes so dark I thought I was going to fall in. I felt dizzy all of a sudden, queasy, and a bit afraid.

'How dare you say that about Aidan,' she said. 'How dare you.'

My throat was as dry as an old stick. 'Sorry,' I told her at last, awkwardly.

'You should be.' Picking my limp fingers off her arm, she tossed her hair and stormed off.

God, what I have to put up with.

All I could do was follow, but she was small and quick and most of all she was angry. Ducking and swerving, she could nip through crowds of shoppers where I could only barge, shove and mutter belated apologies I didn't mean. I was jogging now but I could barely keep her in sight, let alone catch her.

A gang of Reservoir Puppies swaggered across her path, but they were distracted by the burgers they were shoving in their faces and they let her through with a few remarks I'm glad I couldn't hear. When they caught sight of me, their heads came up and their shoulders hunched forward, like something out of Big Ape Diary. Eyeballs swivelled to each other and to me, wondering if it was worth it, but I eyed them hard, then cut my eyes away deliberately, hands in pockets, forward momentum maintained. I'm not looking for trouble but I'll give you some if you ask nicely.

They thought about blocking my way, then changed their minds. Didn't get out of the way, as such, but they rearranged their choreography, slick and unconcerned, and somehow a path opened through so I wouldn't have to shoulder any of them and they wouldn't have to respond. We all have our pride. And you have to be in the mood to look for trouble. And anyway, it was lunchtime.

Allie had a terrific start on me now but I knew most of her evasive ploys and I knew she'd most likely head for the retail estate. It was on the edge of the town and she liked that; she didn't like hanging around the streets. The streets of town meant more people. But beyond the retail warehouses and the railway line and the wasteland of billboards, the town petered out, turning into something you couldn't quite call the countryside: broken fences, fields full of ragwort and willowherb, rusting car bodies and coils of discarded wire. A thin burn leaked through it, its edges marked by beige scum and torn plastic bags. Hardly the stuff of poetry but it suited Allie. No buildings, apart from one derelict shack and a filthy caravan tipped over on one wheel. Dad would have liked it here too. No people. No trouble.

I couldn't blame her for liking it, but I wished she'd go the long way round to get there. I wished she wouldn't clamber along the sides of the railway cutting, where weeds grew thick, where you couldn't see rusting barbed wire or broken posts that might trip you and send you tumbling down the slope on to the tracks. I wished she'd slog down to the level crossing half a mile away like everybody else, but Allie didn't ever take the long way round. She didn't like the road. Houses backed on to it on one side, their long gardens blocked from the road by high fences. On the other side was the railway itself, sunk into a cutting, the rails emerging from a dark tunnel and converging far in the distance at the level crossing. The road was dingy and quiet, and in winter it was staggeringly ill-lit. I wasn't keen on it myself.

Halting now at the tunnel mouth and the cutting, I knew Allie had come this way again. A new swathe had been cut through the undergrowth, zigzagging down to the line, the stems broken, cotton-fluff seeds drifting in air. I started to clamber, hesitantly and sideways, the gradient jolting my knees. The ground beneath my feet was treacherous sand and stone, litter-strewn and weed-choked beneath the scrub. It took me longer than Allie to get to the foot of the slope. Always did, which was another reason she came this way. I felt like a coward but I wasn't going any faster.

I stopped three-quarters of the way to the bottom of the embankment and squinted up the line. Shimmering with distance, the little white sticks that were the level-crossing barriers sighed into place to block the road. No point going any further, then. I was not crossing the tracks, not now. I slumped among the tangled stalks and waited for the song.

It must have been something about the long gradual curve of the tunnel, or maybe the depth of the cutting. It muffled the song to a soft hum that was more a feeling than a sound, a sensation in your bones and nerves. More the nerves in my case.

Idly I pulled the white fluff off a dying stalk, let it drift in the windless day towards the rails. I thought the wisps hovered and trembled, but it might have been my imagination. I glanced up at the level crossing again, so far away, too far for a lazy girl to walk. Railways make everything distant. You look along them like you're looking into another world and one you'll never reach. It's something to do with those parallel shining lines, converging, converging and never meeting. Infinity. Eternity.

Too big to get your head around, anyway. I lay back on my elbows. Anyone watching would have thought I was relaxing, cool as anything, but I was lying back so that there was more of me in contact with the earth, so that my fingers could curl round the coarse grass weeds and anchor me to the world. The singing was louder now, and soon the bass roar of the train would harmonise with its own echo, drown its own song . . .

Soon? Now. *Then.*

It came howling out of the tunnel mouth like a demon. I blinked fast so I could catch instants of lives behind my eyelids. An infant at the window, mother's hands on its waist; a lanky girl gazing into a laptop; men, women, balanced like dancers, bums against seatbacks and folded papers in one hand. But the instants were only that, and they were gone.

Honestly, there are people who do not understand how fast they are. It's not like taking your life in your hands and running across a motorway, say. That's fast but it's not *this* fast. That would be stupid, but this would be suicidal. It would be taking your life in your hands and chucking it on to the tracks and leaving it there. All broken.

I've always been afraid of the trains. Maybe it comes from watching them when I was very little, and thinking they were some kind of gods. Almost the first thing I read, when I learned to read, was the sign that said *Beware of Trains.* So I took the sign for a sign. I took it at its word. And I have never stopped being wary of the trains.

Allie had never been frightened of the trains, which was stupid of her, but at least she treated them with a healthy respect. After all, she too listened for the song. I could only trust that she'd never cross the tracks in the cutting when she heard the singing begin.

I waited till the song had faded, and that was a long time. It had to fade away to nothing, because I wouldn't move till I knew there wasn't another voice singing behind it, harmonising in a treacherous hum so you wouldn't hear it till it broke into its own roar and hit you. I waited till the silence was more than silence, till it was a whole vacuum of sensation and sound, then sidestepped down the embankment once more. It did occur to me to trudge all the way down to the level crossing, but the little white sticks had lifted, and cars were trundling over. Besides, when I checked my watch I knew I was in enough trouble already.

I bolted across the tracks, trying to forget my phobia about catching a foot between the rails or under a sleeper, and scrambled up the other side. Allie wasn't far away; in fact, when I got to the top of the embankment she was just on the other side, halfway down the shallow hill, arms hunched round her knees, fidgeting guiltily as I slumped at her side.

'I'm sorry, Nick,' she said, before I could get an angry word in edgeways.

I sighed. 'Allie . . .'

'It was wrong, what I did. I'm sorry.'

'Which bit?' I said bitterly.

She didn't answer me for a while. In the ragged field below us, a pale sun glinted on a boggy patch that marked the feeble burn. Dirty twigs bare of leaves hung limply over its banks, garlanded with plastic bags and streamers of God-knew-what. It was pretty in a way.

'I couldn't go to school,' said Allie, 'because it's the anniversary and the teachers were talking about some kind of ceremony, and I couldn't stand it. But Aidan was angry with me. So I went out robbing things to annoy him.'

Something unpleasant walked up my spine, like a spider under my skin.

'But I'm sorry I came across the railway. I shouldn't've done that. I knew you were after me and once I got here I was worried about you. You did wait for the train?'

'Course I did,' I said. 'You didn't.'

'It wasn't singing when I came.'

'Allie,' I said. I rubbed my arms to make them feel warmer. 'Allie, if you heard the trains singing. And if you were running. And if Aidan said, well, run anyway, run and you'll make it before the train comes . . .'

'Yeah?'

'Well, Allie, would you just run? Would you run across if Aidan told you to?'

She smiled at me. The faintest breeze wisped a blunt

lock of hair across her face and I used my forefinger to push it back behind her ear. Then I picked willowherb fluff out of her hair. She was still smiling when I did all this and I wished she'd just stop smiling and answer me.

'Nick,' she said at last. 'Nick, Aidan would never tell me to do that.'

'But if he did?'

She pushed my hand gently away from her hair, and rearranged it herself, and then she tipped her head back to smile at the invisible boy leaning against her shoulder.

'Aidan would never do anything to hurt me,' she said. 'Would you, Aidan?'

She wouldn't go back to school with me, and I didn't feel I could leave her, so that was it: I was for it. I tried not to think about it; at least I tried to think only about Allie, who would not get into much trouble. If I explained, I might not either. It was just that I felt too tired and too ground down and too hacked off with the world to bother explaining myself. So I just took Allie home (and Aidan now that she'd found him), and later that afternoon I went back to the seventh circle of hell to retrieve my stuff from my locker, hoping I wouldn't be noticed.

I am never Not Noticed, I'm too big and ugly. And sod's law being what it is, McCluskey was standing right there in the corridor outside his office as I sloped in. I did the eye-contact trick with the big fascist, hoping that like a one-man hostile gang he'd let me pass, but it was a non-starter.

'Oy, *Geddes*.'

I thought about pretending I'd gone deaf, but he'd only snarl at me in sign language. I wondered how he'd sign an obscenity, an earful of sarcasm and another final warning. Be interesting to find out, but instead I let him bawl me into the deputy head's office.

He was quieter with the door shut. 'Would you care to explain yourself, Geddes?'

Oh, he was going to be elaborately polite. That was a bad sign.

'I don't understand you. You don't have to be here.'

Oh, aye, and leave Allie to the hyenas? It was bad enough with me around, and I didn't plan to find out how it would go for her if I wasn't.

I couldn't be bothered explaining this to McCluskey, so I gave him the Withering Look of Dumb Insolence.

'Oh, you're past this crap, aren't you, Geddes?' His weary sigh of boredom made my stomach twist and jerk. The shame was unexpected and a little painful. I didn't let it bother me.

'Sixth year, Geddes. That makes you almost a grown-up.' There was a sneer in his voice. 'Sixth years are in school of their own free will, *boy*. If your free will can't be bothered to turn up, get another life. Go flip a burger.'

A bit more along those lines, and he let me go. I got the impression he was trying to needle me into a reaction, but I was better than that. All I had to do was stomach a year. All I had to do was protect my sister. Oh, and turn around my whole life and my educational prospects. Piece of piss. I didn't have to be liked. Not by McCluskey and not by anybody else.

Just as well, really.

Slouching home, miserable and furious, I wished I'd dragged Allie back to school to share the bollocking. But then, nobody yelled at Allie. Even if I'd hauled her back by the hair – even tomorrow, if she deigned to turn up – nobody would. They'd probably offer the brat more counselling.

At times like this, the only company I could bear was Lola Nan's. I reckon that was because Lola Nan's world made no sense at all, and sometimes mine didn't either. She and I used to connect; we liked each other a lot. Perhaps, on some level, we still did.

Or maybe I was kidding myself, but as I creaked open the rusting gate of our house I felt a desperate longing to see her, to bask for a while in her irrational, largely silent company. Lola Nan didn't ask awkward questions (apart from, occasionally, 'Where's Geoffrey?' – Granda having retired to his crematorium urn twenty years ago).

When I was little, Lola Nan used to half sing, half hum to me to calm me down and stop me crying. Nowadays there was no singing but often she still hummed, tunelessly and for hours on end, and I found that just as comforting as I always had.

Anyway, I'd had such a bad day I didn't deserve for it to get any worse. But it went right ahead and did, because when I got home and slammed the door and went into the sitting room, Lola Nan wasn't there.

But Aidan's mother was.

3

There was nothing imaginary about Aidan's mother.
Often it seemed she was on the verge of being imaginary,
even to herself. But not yet. Not yet.

She and Mum were sitting opposite one another, Mum
in Lola Nan's stained armchair and Aidan's mother in the
best one. They held cups of tea, a biscuit perched on each
saucer. Neither biscuit had been touched, so each was
melting in a little crescent of chocolate against the hot
china. Lola Nan must have been banished upstairs for the
duration.

The two women turned simultaneously as I pushed
open the door, Mum with an expression of faint panic
that wasn't quite hidden by her sensible counsellor-of-
the-heart exterior. Aidan's mum wore her regular smile.

She had a broad, bright and pretty face and she smiled a
lot. She wasn't just brittle, she was already broken and

she looked like she was held together only by an act of will. You got the feeling that if she stopped concentrating for a single second she'd disintegrate like some clever special effect, that we'd have to hoover the bits off the carpet like so much shattered china.

I liked Aidan's mum, and I felt sorry for her, sorry that she had to put up with Allie's nonsense, but I could hardly say so.

It wasn't as if Allie was discreet. One day the poor woman had come upon my sister in the park, sitting on a bench hugging her knees and talking to thin air. Allie hadn't even had the decency to lie about her invisible friend's identity. The invisible friend's mother had fled home in silent tears.

'Hello, Nick.' Sunk in the armchair, Aidan's mum gave me her bright and fragile smile. She always tried hard to be civil and friendly to me and I appreciated that.

'Hello,' I said, and then, 'Is it Allie?'

'Nick,' said Mum, perfectly illustrating the expression 'covered in embarrassment'. Mum may be chock-full of words of wisdom, but God, she's sometimes stuck for them.

'I know Allie's a bit old for this,' Mum managed at last. 'I know that, we know that. She should have outgrown it by now.'

Aidan's mum looked at the floor, at the incredibly clean bit of carpet where Lola Nan had been doing the hoovering. 'Well, we understood, you see. We understood at the beginning. It's her way of coping, isn't it?'

But she wouldn't be here if they still understood. She wouldn't be here if it was still OK.

'I wish I could talk to her.' Mum rubbed her temples manically.

'I can see it's hard,' said Aidan's mum.

'She's had counselling. The psychologist, he said it was best not to rush it, not to force her. He's not seen this before. He thinks maybe . . . the shock. You know?'

'I know,' said Aidan's mum.

That encouraged Mum. 'He doesn't think she's *pretending*. He says maybe she made herself believe it. That he's really there. And eventually she'll . . . she'll just accept he isn't. You see? Her mind's created Aidan and it'll . . . you know . . . uncreate him.'

I looked at Aidan's mum. I was thinking, Someone already uncreated him. I bet she was thinking that too, but she didn't say it.

'It's . . . we mustn't try to . . . rush it,' Mum finished lamely.

Aidan's mum stared at the wall. 'It's a bit out of hand,' she blurted. 'That's all. It's been a year now and she isn't even . . . she isn't . . .'

'Family,' I suggested.

She swallowed, so embarrassed and shamefaced that I wanted to pat her shoulder and tell her it wasn't her fault. I think Aidan's mum spent half her life trying to make other people feel less awkward about what had happened, trying to put them at their ease.

At last she cleared her throat and said, 'You see, it's upsetting Orla.'

It was upsetting Orla.

'I'll talk to Allie,' I said.

Mum looked at me like I was Sir Gawain of the Round Table or something. The saintly one. Him. 'Really, Nick? But are you sure it's a good –'

'It's upsetting Orla,' I said. I looked at the wall too. I could see why Aidan's mum found it so fascinating. 'I mean, I'll just talk to her. See what she says. Y'know.' I was embarrassed now. 'Not promising anything. You know how she is.'

'I'd appreciate it, Nick.' Aidan's mum – *Orla's* mum – smiled at me and I thought, Yup. This was a good move. Then I felt really rubbish for thinking that.

'That's kind of you,' she went on. 'I know it's difficult.'

'Um, yeah,' I said. 'OK.'

I don't know why I said I'd do it. Well, I do know: it was to get me brownie points with Orla, to shorten somewhat the odds against getting her naked underneath me, so it was hardly altruistic. But given that those odds were so ridiculously long, it was as heroic a gesture as I could manage. Heroic and futile and self-sacrificing, I told myself as I climbed the stairs with a heavy heart. I'd do it for Orla.

Self-sacrificing, my backside. Self-*obsessed*. And it was nothing to do with my backside; it was my groin, which just ached with frustrated love, and I had to do something to take my mind off it. Or rather – since my mind had little to do with it – something to advance my cause, if only by the tiniest margin.

I hesitated outside Allie's open bedroom door. She was hunched over her computer, her intent face lit by a bluish glow. I didn't think it was a good idea, letting her have a computer in her bedroom with an internet connection and everything, but the trouble with Mum was that she hated falling out with anyone, and the trouble with Allie was that no one liked to upset her.

Allie knew both these vital facts.

Well, so far as I knew she wasn't getting into trouble: not on the internet, anyway. I came into the room and stood behind her, watching the screen, but right now all she was reading was a rugby website.

Rugby, of course, was Aidan's big thing.

My heart hurt my ribs, it was beating so furiously. I was going to have to say something or explode. Orla, I thought. It's all for Orla.

'He's not here, Allie,' I said.

'What?' She didn't turn.

'He's not here. Aidan. He isn't here, OK? Stop it.'

She gave a patient sigh. 'Of course he isn't.'

I was silent for a few seconds. 'He isn't?'

'No. He's downstairs. He wanted to see his mum.'

I should have known better than to hope. I sat on her bed and put my head in my hands, rubbing my scalp ferociously. I wanted to cry and I wanted to laugh. Mostly I wanted to cry. 'Please stop this,' I said again. 'Please.'

'It's not up to me,' said Allie. Her pale face glowed blue and eerie, dark eyes steadily reflecting the screen. I couldn't even see her blink.

'How do you think his mother feels?'

Her white knuckles tensed on the mouse, but calmly she said, 'I don't think. I know.'

It scared me, the way Allie never lost her temper. 'It hurts her, you pretending he's still there.'

'I'm not pretending.'

I ignored that. 'She's really upset. So's Orla.'

'Oh,' said Allie. 'Orla. So that's it.'

I could have hit her, then, for the smug little smile on the side of her face. Curling my fingers into tight fists, I snapped, 'It's a hideous thing to do. You're hurting everybody else to make yourself feel better. You're only thinking about yourself and it's bloody selfish.'

The desktop went over to screensaver, a bleak desertscape, so she couldn't have moved the mouse for a while. In the window behind her desk I could see her face reflected, lit by the screen, her mouth sulky, eyes gleaming with the tears that spilled down her face.

'I know you miss him,' I said.

'I don't miss him.' Her voice was perfectly steady. 'He's still here.'

I got up and stormed out then, I couldn't help it. I stood outside her room fuming and trying not to worry, which is quite a hard combination, but I couldn't face going downstairs yet. I wanted Aidan's mother to leave first so I wouldn't have to admit I'd failed.

Mind you, I don't know what I was supposed to achieve when the professionals had been dismal failures. Allie told them what they wanted to hear – something she was good at – and went home from every appointment still attached to Aidan's invisible hip. I was sick of not challenging her. Angry, too. I suppose I thought one day I'd just say 'Stop it' and because she was my little sister and I loved her, she would stop it, just for me.

It hadn't happened yet. Much as I loved her, that did make me wonder if she loved me back. If she still loved me, I thought sometimes, aching with self-pity and righteous indignation, she'd give up Aidan – who didn't after all exist – so that I could have Orla, who did.

I don't know how the mothers were managing the awkward pause till I reappeared. They'd never been particular friends and Mrs Mahon was here only to try to sort out Allie. Maybe she was desperately killing time till she finished her tea and her half-melted biscuit. I got the feeling that's what she did with a lot of her time. Tried desperately to kill it.

I toed open the door of Lola Nan's bedroom. She was perched on the edge of her bed, tensed like a rabbit in headlights, staring at the wall. 'She won't be long, Lola Nan,' I said. 'I think Mrs Mahon's going soon. You can go back down in a minute.'

She was doing that thing again, patting the air. Crouching, I caught her hand. I smiled at her, even though her fingers tightened reflexively around mine and she was just about breaking the bones. Tears glittering in her washed-out eyes, she opened her mouth and made sucking sounds, as if she was experimenting with saying something. Then her eyes swam into focus, her brows dipped together and she hollered at me.

'We were talking! Private! Go away!'

Then she screamed, incoherently, screamed till her eye sockets darkened and her papery skin rippled and her electric-shock hair quivered with the effort.

I sighed and stood up, prising off her hand. Who was she talking to? Bloody Granda? Hell, I thought, if Allie can have an imaginary friend, why not Lola Nan? She was probably more in need of one, and Lola Nan wasn't breaking anybody's heart. There was no point taking offence. After all, an illness wasn't a personal insult. Sometimes I was afraid a small real Lola Nan was inside that head, battering her fists against her cage. I could imagine her ricocheting around inside her empty skull, bouncing off the bone walls like a crazy pinball lost in the machine, howling in frustration, and that was why she sometimes yelled and howled at me.

But probably not. She was probably dead already, the Lola Nan who used to take me on her lap and sing and hum like the rails, before she went off them.

I crept on to the landing and bent over the banisters.

The women were in the hallway, and I could hear about half their murmured words. Most were Mum's, and I have to say I was impressed. She comforts for a living, after all; she could comfort for her country, and she was saying the sort of things to Mrs Mahon that I never could. If she was good at nothing else, she was good at sympathising, and I felt a reluctant embarrassed pride.

Then she blew it.

She touched Aidan's mum's upper arm and Aidan's mum tried hard not to flinch, because if she was anything like Orla she didn't like gratuitous touching. (Luckily I hadn't yet made the mistake of trying, but I'd been witness to a nasty incident with Kev Naughton.) Mum must have sensed resistance, because she let go of Mrs Mahon's arm. On an afterthought, she snatched the woman's hand and gave it a comforting squeeze.

'Remember,' said Mum, 'God never gives us a burden greater than we can bear.'

It was one of her favourites. I'd heard it before, on Words of Utterly Fatuous Folk-Wisdom, and I'd thought it a clunker even then. Now I shut my eyes and gripped the banister rail, hoping I wasn't going to be tipped over by the dizzying wave of shame.

Sometimes a parent says something so embarrassing you want to die. And sometimes dying just isn't enough: you want to kill the parent too. That was it for me. Mum explaining to a dead boy's mother that her nebulous God didn't actually have it in for her; he was only playing some cosmic game of Buckaroo. And presumably, when Aidan's devastated dad walked out on what was left of his family, God had been a little careless hooking on the Stetson.

Aidan's mum never let on, though. I suppose she was too polite and she didn't want Mum to feel awkward. I couldn't see her face but I suppose she just smiled at Mum and walked quietly out and closed the door. When her blurred shadow was gone from the patterned glass and her car door had clunked shut and the engine coughed, purred and faded, Mum put her face in her hands and started to cry.

I left her to it.

THEN

4

Kevin Naughton killed him. Kevin Naughton killed my sister's boyfriend with a Valu-Pack Stay-Sharp vegetable knife; he stuck it in the brother of the girl I love and severed his subcostal artery. Kevin Naughton murdered Aidan Mahon.

Kevin Naughton was my friend.

What were you thinking? Dad would scream at me in the days afterwards. *Why did you get involved with that scum? What the hell were you thinking?*

Quite, Dad. What was I thinking? You may well ask.

I like to tell myself that when your mother does the local Whatever-God-You-Fancy slot – and occasionally uses you to illustrate a twee point about her amusing family life – you have to be meaner, tougher and sicker than anyone else, or you're dead. And there's an element of truth in that.

It's complicated, though.

I first laid eyes on Kev Naughton on my first day at Craigmyle High. I knew right away he was as scared as the rest of us newcomers, but what he was most scared of was his big brother. Mickey Naughton was a lot older and he'd left school, but he liked to keep an eye on Kev. He had a job selling bull semen to farmers – the back of his car was full of little tubes of spunk – but he must have picked some irregular hours for impregnating cows, because it left Mickey plenty of time to loiter near the school and monitor Kev's progress.

Maybe it was his intimate involvement with cattle; maybe over-familiarity had bred contempt. Mickey Naughton wanted to stay at the top of the food chain, and he wanted Kev up there with him. Naughton family values were Darwinian, smart and cold. Just like Mickey.

I was dead impressed with Mickey.

Yes, he was a scary bastard. Charming and all, but then I think the charm was part of the fear factor. I couldn't imagine Mickey taking crap from anyone, bureaucrat or traffic warden or snotty neighbour. I bet no kid would ever dare pee in Mickey's garden and run away laughing. Mickey would never quarrel with his boss over something pointless; he wouldn't clamber up on to his dignity and fall off. Mickey did not smell faintly of stale wine, and he did not wear a ponytail or the T-shirts of his lost youth. Mickey was dapper, with a nice line in shirts and jackets. Mickey had a white dazzling smile and no tattoos. I used to look at Mickey – nervously, out of the corner of my eye – and think, now that's what I call a role model.

Besides, my dad never saved me from getting the crap kicked out of me.

Exhibit A in my dodgy defence: Calum Sinclair. Let's take Calum Sinclair into consideration.

I was never that friendly with Calum at primary, but at Craigmyle High, for the first few weeks, we gravitated together. We came from the same part of town. Our parents knew each other vaguely. We liked the same films, we liked the same games, we pretty much liked the same music. I'd given him half the songs on his iPod, so I suppose I took it personally when some thick ape from third year tried to take it off him.

We were outside the school gates but it was a quiet time of day and the two of us were backed up against the wire fence. Josh the Ape wasn't that bright but he had a reputation, and large friends, two of whom flanked him as he held out his hand for the iPod, making beckoning motions with his fingers. I scowled at him.

Calum wasn't scowling; Calum, from the look of him, was about to soil himself. There were tears of fury in his eyes, but he was about to hand over the iPod, I could see his hand going to his pocket. I couldn't believe what I was not-quite-seeing.

'Don't give it to him!' I blurted, and one of the side-apes grabbed me by the throat and kicked my knee hard. I went half down, my leg crumpling, but now I was as mad as a cat with a firework up its arse. Calum had frozen in terror, so I lurched for his arm and grabbed it to stop him giving away the iPod. I got kicked in the side for that, which made me lose my grip. Calum was knocked down and away from me, and it took two kicks in his belly before he was shoving the iPod at them, gasping and squeaking at them to take the frigging thing.

Understandably, they did.

They were still kind of enjoying themselves, so they set to with a bit more kicking and punching – well, what passed for punching with a pack of rock apes – and I was roaring and whacking them back when one of them was yanked off me and thrown back.

'Oy,' said Mickey Naughton. 'Piss off out of here.'

They were about to, and no hanging about, when he added: 'And give us that.'

Meekly one of them handed over the iPod, and they scarpered.

Mickey didn't hand over Calum's property, but turned it in his fingers. I was still panting and snarling with rage. I looked at Calum, expecting some sort of reflection of myself. Instead, there was only familiar, tearful, impotent fury. My stomach went cold. If you stuck a ponytail on him, and twenty years, and a Jeff Buckley T-shirt . . .

Smiling, Mickey dangled the iPod by its earphone cord. 'Whose is it?'

'His,' I said, jerking my head at Calum.

'Oh, aye?' He looked from me to Calum and back again. 'If it wis yours I'd give it back. You're the one that wis fighting for it.'

I was still enraged enough to say, 'Give it to him.'

Mickey tilted an eyebrow. 'Seeing as *you're* asking.' He tossed it disdainfully to Calum, and winked at me. 'You're a good lad.'

I was sweating and wiping blood off my nose and gasping for breath, but what I remember most clearly about that moment is my whole body puffing up with macho pride as Mickey walked away without a backward glance. I turned to Calum. Maybe I was expecting a little admiration. Maybe I was expecting a little gratitude.

Oh, aye. I was forgetting he'd suddenly turned into a clone of my dad. The only expression on his bruised face was resentment.

'What did you do that for?' he snapped.

I was speechless.

'It's only a frigging iPod,' he yelled, though tears brimmed at the corner of his eyes. 'You don't fight back! Everybody says that. They might have had a knife or something!'

I stared, fascinated, as he stormed off.

My dad threw hissy fits *just* like that.

You don't fight back. Right. I'd better remember that. I didn't get these life lessons at home. Except, of course, by watching.

I kept right on watching. I wasn't committing myself,

not in these early weeks, though Kevin Naughton was suddenly trying to be my best friend. He shouted out to me in the playground, asked me where I went to primary school, which teams and bands did I like, what did I think about *her* or *them* or *that*? He flattered me with questions I'm sure he knew the answers to already.

'My brother thinks you're great,' he'd say. And I'd think about Mickey, so cool and couldn't-give-a-damn, so smart and professional, so brutal and frightening. I should have been wary. Instead I was chuffed out of my skull.

Meanwhile, Calum was giving me the cold shoulder, and I realised I didn't care, especially when it clicked that he was now a little scared of me. Truly, I did not go to school with the intention of getting into the wrong crowd. I did not pack my fall-from-grace into my backpack on day one. But I'd heard Craigmyle High chewed you up and spat you out, and many things determined what shape you were when you sat dazed in the pool of its spittle at the end of your school career. Teachers were the least of it.

I intended to remain human; well, humanoid. Nick-shaped. I wasn't going to be stamped into something unrecognisable or even, God forbid, something Dad-shaped. Like my ex-friend Calum . . .

You don't fight back. Well, well. There was a lesson that worked two ways.

I'd like to be one of life's good guys, who wouldn't? But I was not going to be one of its victims. I was not going to be humiliated and bullied every day of my life, then go home with the shame simmering in my embittered heart and take it out on my kids. I was not going to be small that way. I was never going to grow a tragic ponytail just so people could pull it.

Don't get me wrong: the first time my dad hit me really was the last time, but I'll never forget the red shame and rage in his eyes. I was eleven: it was my last day of primary and I suppose I was a bit full of myself.

Dad had fallen out with Mum, in the wake of an argument with his boss. He was always having those, and he always wound himself up to the point where he threatened to leave if he didn't *get a little more respect around here*. Since his long line of employers must have found that demand as impossible as I did, it always ended the same way: a month's notice and a P45. Well, it had happened again, and I suppose Dad was in no mood to be looked at the wrong way. It's what happens when you let the world sit on you too long.

I was shocked at the time, though. I was shocked by his expression, by the smell of midday whisky, and most of all when he spun round and his knuckles connected with my cheekbone just below my eye socket. I was so astonished I didn't even feel the pain to begin with. I didn't hit him back and I didn't run away; I just couldn't believe he'd done it to me, and all because I'd made a stupid unfunny joke about getting a season ticket to the Job Centre. Too near the knuckle, I suppose: for him and, as it turned out, for me. He stood there until he couldn't look at me any longer and his eyes hunted all over the room for something else to focus on. He mumbled an apology and we told Mum I fell downstairs. He never smelt of whisky at lunchtime again and he never hit me again. I never let him. I was never going to let anyone hit me again.

I'd promised myself that, and now, many months on, I'd proved it. The respect of people like Mickey and Kev, I discovered, was a lot more gratifying than respect from the likes of Calum.

So the survival instinct I was born with was by now very well honed. What's more, I was always tall for my age, I was always well built, and I always had menacing eyes. That isn't my fault, but never look a gift gene in the mouth, and I knew if I threw in my lot with Kev Naughton I'd be fine. I'd be protected from the lesser thugs of life, and I was sure I'd be of use to Kev. And I was.

But like I said: it's complicated.

I thought it was a game, the way you do when you're twelve. I didn't exactly think it was play-acting but I was starring in my own little movie and the sad thing is I wasn't even a headline act. Kev swaggered and bullied; he threatened and intimidated, but he was also funny, and he could be surprisingly kind if he wasn't concentrating on being an arse. I didn't think he was all that bad, and to be honest I thought he needed protecting from himself.

So here's how it happens. Here's how it happened for *me*.

You start by sorting out people you don't like, people nobody likes. Other smaller yobs and bullies. You teach them a lesson. You and your pals aren't bullies: you're the Three Musketeers, the Fantastic Four, the League of Extraordinary Gentlemen.

It's all too easy. You get the better of someone and you like the feel of it so much, you want that feeling again. You want no one ever to get the better of *you*.

So you wake up one day and you're the arbiter of morality, the arbiter of cool. Now you're punishing people for things that wouldn't have shown up on your radar a week ago: wearing the wrong trainers, liking the wrong music, carrying the wrong phone, giving you the wrong kind of look. In the end you're doing it for your image, your status, your pride.

Just for the hell of it.

I suppose Kev was like me. He was thinking Vinnie Jones or Samuel L Jackson: more anti-hero than villain. He didn't want to be the guy who gets splattered in the second scene; he wanted to be there when the credits rolled. DVDs, I tell you: God's apology for you being born too late, God's way of letting you catch up on all those films you missed.

Kev might have liked to be one of life's heroes too, but not Mickey. Mickey Naughton wasn't like Kev, but then he wasn't like anyone I'd ever met. He had places to go in the world and he was smart, well dressed, charming to little old ladies and no doubt to frustrated Friesians too. Mickey's boss thought the world of him.

Mickey Naughton was an evil shit.

When I saw him beat the crap out of his little brother, that was my tipping point. I could have tipped one way or the other, I suppose. I hadn't made up my mind. I still had time to save my soul, to be one of the good guys, one of the victims, one of the losers.

I'm not sure what Kev had done and I never liked to ask him, but I don't think it was all that serious. Mickey was still knocking him into shape, that was all. Maybe Kev had chickened out of a challenge, maybe he'd failed to deliver a message or tried to keep a stolen phone for himself, or maybe he'd just answered his brother back on a bad day. Whatever, I turned the corner on my way home and there they were, in the copse of sickly trees where a footpath wavered alongside the school wall.

When a computer superstore was built next to the school, the council made them keep that copse of trees because it had Amenity Value. I wish they'd just concreted it over and extended the car park, because what it really has is Ambush Value, Assault-and-Battery Value. A quiet green space like that is asking for trouble, and that was what Kev was getting.

I didn't feel I had to run. I stood like a lemon, and Mickey took no notice of me whatsoever, just went on slapping Kev's face, coolly and deliberately. Kev was crying but his lips were clamped hard together so he wouldn't make a sound. On his school trousers there was a dark stain where he'd wet himself. With good reason, as it turned out, because when Mickey had finished slapping him, he took hold of Kev's head and brought it snapping down on to his raised knee, then kicked him in the stomach and left him curled on the ground. A dog walker appeared, ambling down the far end of the footpath, quite a tall middle-aged guy, but when he saw us he turned on his heel and hurried away in the opposite direction, dragging a yapping Jack Russell that was obviously keener for a scrap than he was.

Mickey took no notice of the walker or the dog. He smoothed his hair and dusted a speck of bark off his jacket before hooking it over his shoulder. As he passed me he paused, put a hand on my shoulder and smiled.

'You're a clever lad, Nick. Smarter than he is. Tougher and all.' The hand patted my shoulder lightly. 'Take care of him, eh? He needs looking after.'

I was too shocked to say a word, but Mickey didn't wait for one. He got back into his company Mondeo and drove away.

When he'd gone I hovered near Kev, not at all sure he'd want me around but not quite willing to leave him there alone. A tiny whimper seemed to be coming from another dimension, but I suppose it was coming from Kev. When he saw my feet he fell silent, eyes burning with tears, jaw clenched with humiliated rage. There was a stain of reddish purple on his cheekbone and eye socket that was going to be a lovely bruise. I'd never seen anything so pathetic and vulnerable.

'Y'all right?'

'Aye. Fine.' He half sat up, spat out a gobbet of blood.

'What did you do?'

He gave me a wary look. 'S'fine. Nothing. I was cheeky. Asking for it.'

'Oh, aye?'

'It wis *my fault*. I'm fine. Listen, you, don't go and tell . . .'

'Nah. Course.' I liked the way he wasn't whingeing. Taking a bit of responsibility, too.

Still, I was smarter than Kev was, and that was official. Tougher, as well. He needed looking after. His brother had told me so. His evil, cool, clever brother.

I glanced at the deserted footpath, then at the road. Then I turned back to Kev.

'It'll be fine,' I said.

I meant: I won't tell anyone, and no one's coming, and nobody else saw.

But I also meant: we need each other. We can use each other. I'll look out for you.

And that's how I sold my soul to the devil.

I never saw Kev brought that low again. Whatever he'd done wrong he didn't repeat it, instead applying himself with determination to becoming the man his brother wanted him to be. By his third year he was big and mean enough to intimidate most of the school, including a lot of older kids and half the teachers. He didn't scare McCluskey, obviously, and I don't think he scared the head either, but only because the Brain pretended he didn't exist. I became Kev's principal bodyguard, henchman and enforcer, and while I'm not proud of it, I survived and my phone never got nicked. It's a jungle out there.

Mickey still gave Kev a whack now and again, to keep him on his toes, but I'd seen enough of the man's explosive rages to keep out of his way. I stayed out of the line of fire and I tried to make sure Kev did too, because Mickey could turn from cool charm to apocalyptic fury in the time it took to snap your fingers.

Mickey was the only father figure Kev had, but why would he have wanted another one? Fathers bitch about the neighbours' noise levels, lose the ensuing quarrel to the point of utter humiliation, then get mildly stunned before taking themselves off to bed. It's not as if a father would have controlled either of them. A father might have made things worse. After all, the Naughtons didn't get their violent genes from a fairy godmother.

Mickey wasn't a father figure to me. He wasn't. I wanted to impress him, that was all. That was *all*. I could never forget him dangling that iPod and saying *If it wis yours I'd give it back. You're the one that wis fighting for it. You're a good lad*. The memory could still make me swagger. I wanted to hear it again, or something like it.

That bloody iPod. It was only an iPod: Calum never said a truer word. But *I wis the one that fought for it.*

Must be why I took it back.

I took it back off Calum because, morally speaking, it was mine. If it hadn't been for me, Josh the Ape would have had it long ago, or Mickey would have kept it. Half the songs on it were mine anyway. Calum didn't care enough – about the iPod, about his pride, about anything – to fight for it. I did. I cared.

And you know, *you don't fight back.*

He held out his hand and my fingers closed over it. It was late autumn and I could have waited for the day when I knew he had his after-school chess club. If I'd done that I could have got him alone, on his way home, when the shadows were thick between the pools of street-light. That wasn't how I wanted to do it. For some reason I wanted him humiliated. I wanted to do this outside the school gates, just as the school disgorged a swarm of kids to see it all, while the teachers, distracted, tidied their desks or bolted for their cars, desperate to get out of there. I wanted to do it with my gang watching. I wanted Kev to tell Mickey all about it.

Maybe I didn't want to look in Calum's eyes all by myself.

Not that I felt guilty. Not that I was sorry for Calum. I felt nothing but contempt. He was resentful and hating and afraid. He didn't even have the guts to say no, to say the iPod wasn't mine and I had no right to it. He didn't have the nerve to ask me what had happened to me, though he probably wanted to know. He just handed the frigging thing over, and I was so angry with him for not even trying to argue, I tossed the iPod into Kev's keeping and went for Calum. Big time.

Pure submission. He was a curled-up ball of fear and pain. The longer he refused to fight back, the angrier I got. What was wrong with him? I never thought to ask what was wrong with me, of course, though I was the one punching him to the ground and slamming my fists and feet into his soft stupid flesh. He had his hands over his eyes and I didn't want that. I'd seen fear in his face, and misery, but it wasn't enough, and I desperately wanted to see his eyes again. I lashed my foot into his hand and he snapped it away with a yelp of pain, but curled up again. I wanted his eyes, though, so I fell on him, flailing at his head. Where was that look he'd given Josh the Ape? I wanted that. I wanted to see my dad, hiding there in Calum's eyes. *Come out, come out, Dad, wherever you are . . .*

There was a tight, closed circle of kids round us, and I realised I was loving it. I think I was. I do seem to remember loving it, loving it so much I couldn't stop. Sunil had to make me stop, tearing me off him because I'd been at this for long enough and there was a limit to what even we could get away with. I kicked Calum once more in the balls for luck and staggered back, exhausted with joy.

There was a kid at the front, filming it all on his mobile. With a snarl Sunil ripped the phone out of his hands and stuffed it in his own pocket, and the kid didn't argue. That was because of me, I thought proudly. They were scared. We had the respect of the entire school, me and Kev and Sunil and the rest. I knew what my dazzled audience was thinking, and it made me light-headed. If I could do this to a guy who used to be my friend, they were wondering, what wouldn't I do? So watch out for that guy. Better take care around him. Don't mess with Nick Geddes, no way. No way, José. I swear to God, the voice in my head was slurring into a New Yoik accent.

'Jesus Christ Almighty.'

It was the voice of a disgusted girl, and it cut through the silence, breaking my spell of terror. (I mean, who did I think I was? The Great Lord Sauron?)

Orla Mahon, brutally beautiful, half a dozen books in her arms and her black nails tapping against the covers. Her disdain punctured my swollen pride and drained all the adrenalin out of my body. My crazy high was gone, replaced by dizziness and the beginnings of embarrassment. Her black-edged eyes were locked on me as she chewed her gum, but though she glanced down at Calum with mild pity she made no move to help him. She turned on her heel and stalked away, her friends at her side.

Her younger brother Aidan was the next to leave, and his friends after him. And then they were all backing away, some of them staring at me, some of them staring at Calum's curled body, some of them pretending they'd seen nothing at all. Was I missing something here? I wasn't seeing much admiration or respect. Not even hatred. Just dislike, that was all: dislike seriously muted by fear.

'Not really supposed to kill the wee fecker,' said Sunil, 'but he was asking for it.'

'Yeah. Good man,' said Kev approvingly, tossing the iPod back to me.

Somehow Kev's approval didn't thrill me. I wondered if even Mickey's meant quite as much as this. I wasn't sure Calum had asked for it really. The boy was crawling to his feet and limping away while he thought he had the chance. I couldn't watch that, couldn't even look at him any more, so I turned away.

And saw Allie.

I thought I was hallucinating. At exactly the same instant I remembered her telling me that she wanted to meet me after school. She wanted to show me something. The memory kicked me in the stomach and I swore, out loud, but somehow didn't manage to make a sound.

She made no sound either. Her dark eyes found mine and wouldn't let go, but she didn't speak. She took one step back, and then another. She turned and walked straight into the road, making a Vauxhall brake and screech and blare its horn, but she didn't flinch. Only at the far side of the road did she start to run.

'Allie!' I yelled.

Aye, like she was going to change her mind and come back. I ran after her, but she did not want to be caught, and she wasn't.

When I got home, exhausted and terrified, she wasn't there. Dad shouted after me as I pelted up the stairs. Something about, where was Allie and wasn't she supposed to be meeting me?

I couldn't even answer him. I ran to the upstairs bathroom, knelt on the lilac shagpile thing round the base of the toilet, gripped the matching lilac-shagpile-covered seat and threw up.

I wasn't Nick-shaped, I was Kev-shaped. I put my head in my hands and looked at the lilac shagpile and threw up again.

NOW

5

I thought Aidan's mum's visit might spark Allie's conscience, might at least shame her into being more discreet. Not a chance. Two days later it was Lola Nan's birthday weekend. Lola Nan's birthday at the beach was a family tradition. So naturally, bloody Aidan had to come too.

It was a stupid tradition to start with, and in the last few years it had become even stupider, even before Allie brought along her imaginary boyfriend. Lola Nan came from a generation that thought it was the best fun imaginable to sit on a bleak beach with sand whisking into your eyes, gulls mugging you for food and the wind-chill factor giving you the skin of a lizard. Dad prodded at the disposable barbecue, as if poking the sausages with a stick would make them cook faster and taste edible. His eyes kept drifting to the cool box, and eventually so did his hand. Needless to say, the sausages got burnt.

Mum was buttering rolls. Shielding her eyes against nonexistent sunlight so she wouldn't quite have to look at me, she called brightly, 'Nick, would you like to help Dad?'

I pretended I didn't hear her. So did Dad. He went on stabbing sausages, and I turned back to Lola Nan. The broad beach was almost deserted but I could get away with selective deafness because Lola Nan and I were higher up a dune, with forest at our back and the whole silky curve of the sea to admire in silence. Mum had wanted her closer to the barbecue, on the flat sand, but I'd insisted they put her here. Lola Nan and I had a nice view. It was only slightly marred by the figures of Mum and Dad and the drifting barbecue smoke.

I was sprawled next to Lola Nan's folding chair. It was one of those canvas jobs with little pockets in the side for your drink. I had a beer I'd filched from the cool box (not that Dad could have objected to me having alcohol, morally speaking, but he was kind of possessive with it). Lola Nan had orange juice, diluted, in a non-spill toddler cup.

I hated them for it.

She didn't seem to mind, though. In her floral dress and floppy white hat she looked vaguely happy, murmuring incoherently as she watched the waves tumble in, the gangster gulls squabble and dive. I suppose she was enjoying herself. Her right hand flapped above the chair's canvas arm, patting her invisible pocket of air. After a while her head tipped back, her mouth fell open and she started to snore.

I was stuffing a folded towel behind her head, to stop it falling off its fragile wrinkled neck, when Allie ran up our dune and waved a sausage on a roll at me. As Lola Nan's head fell the other way, almost bouncing off her saggy chest, I gave up and took the roll.

Allie grinned. 'I'm freezing. Bloody freezing. Why does Mum insist on doing this?'

As I sat in the sand, she flopped down beside me and wriggled under my arm. I pulled another towel round us both and ripped another bite of the roll. This was great. Just me and Allie and a comatose Lola Nan. No Mum, no Dad and no frigging Aidan.

'I know,' I said. 'And she'll insist on Lola Nan paddling. It'll take all day to get her down there.'

'I'm going to tactfully wander off. No way am I putting my feet in that sea. How does Mum think we all enjoy this?'

'Well, Lola Nan does,' I admitted.

'Suppose.' Allie made a face. 'And *allegedly* it's very bonding. Family-wise.'

'Hah,' I said darkly, watching Dad crack open another bottle.

She spluttered a giggle, stuffed the last bit of roll and sausage into her mouth and dusted sand and crumbs off her hands. 'We're off. Come on, then. See you, Nick.

Enjoy your paddle!'

We're off. *We're* off. See you, Nick. *Come on then.*

Heidcase. Deluded wee cow. Abandoned for a phantom, I threw the rest of my roll towards the sea; a gull caught it in mid-air and was instantly mobbed by three more. Mum had to beat off a couple herself as she wobbled up the beach towards us in sequinned flip-flops.

'Happy birthday, Lola Nan!' On her face was a professional warm smile; in her hands she bore a supermarket birthday cake. A cartoon ballerina in lilac icing. The birthday number had been picked off; you could see the pink-stained shape of 5th in between *Happy* and *Birthday.*

Well. It was a nice thought. Lola Nan wouldn't notice. She jerked awake, mumbling.

'Happy Birthday!' said Mum again, trying to maintain her cheery smile.

'Where's the boy?' Lola Nan gripped the canvas chair arms. 'WHERE'S THE BOY?'

Oh, hell's teeth. 'I'm here, Lola Nan.' I scrambled to my feet and took the cake off Mum. 'Here. Happy Birthday.'

'Hmph.' Like a bumptious toddler she scowled at me, then her face broke open in a big smile. 'Can I have some cake?'

'Course you can. It's your birthday,' I said. Mum had forgotten the knife, of course. I dug my fingers into the cake and quarried out a big piece. Lola Nan grabbed it, delighted.

Out of the corner of my eye I saw Mum's face darken, but she bit her lip and made herself smile.

'You're a good boy,' said Lola Nan through a mouthful of sponge and lilac icing.

Mum's face darkened even more.

'You care about me, don't you?' mumbled Lola Nan. 'Not like *her*. She can't even –'

'Wonder where Allie is?' I yelled brightly. 'She'd like some CAKE too!'

Mum's lower eyelids glittered, a row of tears along each. Shit. 'Allie!' I shouted in desperation.

'Where's the *BOY*?' shouted Lola Nan.

'Here!' I turned back to her, and she gripped my hands like she was trying to pull them off at the wrists.

'Sometimes I just can't . . .' began Mum tearfully.

'ALLIE!' I yelled.

'Coming! Hang on!' She was sprinting along the edge of the water, turning towards the dry sand. Then, just as I thought she was coming to my rescue, she stopped, spun on her heel, hooted with laughter. Crouching, she picked up a handful of sand and flung it.

'Aidan! *Quit it!*'

Mum froze. I froze. Dad dropped the barbecue fork in the sand, and Lola Nan just smiled happily at nothing.

'AiiiDAAAAAN!' shrieked Allie.

'Cake,' said Mum brightly, blinking.

That was the moment I noticed two girls walking along the edge of the sea, and an ugly lurcher-like dog plunging in and out of the waves. I knew that dog, I'd seen it before. Gina's dog. Which would explain why Gina, and the girl with her, had come to a stunned halt and were staring at Allie. The other girl was Orla. She stood there, rigid, as Allie threw sand at her invisible murdered brother, yelling his name and giggling.

After a few seconds Gina grabbed Orla's arm and pulled her back the way they'd come, but as Orla turned, her eyes sought out the rest of us. It was me she looked at. I couldn't see her all that clearly but I felt her laser stare in my spine and the nape of my neck. Swallowing, I took a step towards her. With a dismissive toss of her head she walked away, and I watched her go as I listened to my sister shriek with laughter at a dead boy who wasn't there to laugh back.

Aidan was dead and gone, but Allie would never let him go and there was nothing I could do to make her. I felt sick with guilt and uselessness and insomnia, because I hardly slept for two nights after the family outing. On the Monday I went hunting for Orla to apologise for my sister's behaviour at the beach. At least, that's the reason I gave myself. That was my excuse.

Poor Aidan. We're all using him still.

Orla wasn't hanging around the corridors with her posse; she wasn't outside in the school grounds; eventually I found her just the other side of the wire fence, where we weren't supposed to go (Health and Safety). She was sitting against a half-dead tree on the sloping bank of the burn (which was indeed unhealthy and not very safe). The same burn trickled soddenly through Allie's fields, and it didn't get any more appealing by the time it passed the school. Twenty metres on it was swallowed in a concrete tunnel that was like a whalemouth, jammed with a grille of rusty iron baleen. Plastic bags and fast-food boxes had caught in the hatch, tattered by the sluggish current, laced with dirty foam.

Orla knew I was coming but she didn't look up. Without the posse she didn't seem quite so intimidating, so I clambered down the bank, close enough to read the book's cover. Something by Albert Camus.

'Has that got pictures?' I said.

Lame, and she ignored me as I deserved.

'I saw your mum last week. She came round to ours.'

Orla licked a black-polished fingertip and delicately turned a page.

'I've tried to talk to Allie,' I said.

Orla snapped her book shut, keeping her place with a finger. 'What d'you want, Mister Ambassador? A box of Ferrero Rocher?'

I looked at the book with her finger inside it. I could hardly say, *Well, no, but I was hoping for some sex.*

'Eff off, Nick,' she said, as if reading my mind. Except she didn't say 'Eff' either.

I effed off, because I couldn't think what else to do. I hadn't even turned away before she'd opened her book again and fixed her attention somewhere in the middle of the pages, where the spine was. I was watching her that closely and I knew fine she wasn't reading. There was nothing for me to do, though. I climbed back up the bank and it felt like the final ascent of K2.

At the summit waited a smug-looking sherpa.

'You're going about this all wrong,' said Shuggie, falling into step beside me.

I took a breath to tell him to do what Orla told me, but instead I managed to splutter, 'What?'

'I said you're . . .'

'Yeah, shut up. I mean, what would you know about it?'

'Well,' said Shuggie, 'she's not stupid, that Orla.'

I wondered how hard I could hit him without actually hurting him too much. I wondered if I could get him to take his glasses off first. 'What's that supposed to mean?'

Shuggie sighed as though he was at the limit of his tolerance. 'Women want you to be honest, don't they? Orla thinks you're taking the mickey.'

Orla having bagged the only decent quiet and private spot within a mile of the school, I was forced to sit down on the broken tarmac against the wire fence. I was also forced to endure Shuggie, because he sat right down beside me.

'Honesty,' he said. 'That's what women like. Honesty.'

'And you're the expert.'

'More than you, obviously.' He took off his glasses and began to polish them on the hem of his shirt. That was a temptation. I could swing my arm back now and catch him in his bare face, but I knew I never would. Not Shuggie. I knew I'd never bring myself to hit Shuggie. I was sort of responsible for him; I'd made myself responsible for him quite by accident, and now, like he relished telling me, I was stuck with him. Anyway, I was his only friend, in some loose sense of the word. And vice versa, I suppose.

I watched him rub his glasses methodically, one lens at a time, breathing on them in a finicky, delicate way that should have bugged the hell out of me, but was actually strangely calming. I liked the way he was taking such a ridiculous amount of care and time when the supermarket shirt fabric must have been scratching the lens surface anyway. I liked it that Shuggie was still enough like the rest of us to lose his special lens cleaning cloth and have to use his shirt. Glancing at his intent face, naked and funny and vulnerable without its highbrow horn-rims, I caught myself smiling, and had to force a frown.

I don't know why I put up with him. He turned up like some guru whenever I didn't want his advice. If I did want something from him, such as Allie's whereabouts, he was the most elusive geek on the planet. Any other time I could be swaggering down the corridor, giving the likes of Sunil the evil eye so that nobody would ever in the history of the world think they could get away with having another go at me, and I'd feel this presence and there would be Shuggie, hugging some manual on rocket science or string theory or God knew what. And that would be him attached to my hip for the rest of the day. It was doing nothing for my image. He was a small planet sucked into my irresistible orbit. So how come it didn't work this way with Orla Mahon?

I wished I could ask Lola Nan. I wished I'd remembered to ask her this kind of thing earlier, when she was still capable of answering.

'And how is your nan?' asked Shuggie now. 'I suppose she could be worse.'

That was another annoying thing. The little geek was telepathic, but I was in no mood for one of Shuggie's philosophical lectures. 'Piss off, Shugs,' I snapped. 'What d'you know?'

'Well, what does *she* know? Objectively speaking, she doesn't know anything's wrong, does she? Really, she *could* be worse. Look at my dad.'

I was about to open my mouth and say something vicious but I stopped myself in the nick of time. I'd kind of gone off gratuitous cruelty when I heard the first sick Aidan joke within two weeks of his death.

Shuggie told me once he didn't grieve for his dad, not after he was dead, because he was glad for him and he wished he'd put a pillow over his face in the first place, like his dad asked him to (when Shugs was all of eleven). Maybe it'll be like that for me. Maybe I'll be happy for Lola Nan. Maybe I should do the pillow thing for her, not that she'd ever asked . . .

'Why don't you apologise to her?' said Shuggie.

What? To Lola Nan? In advance? The world swung on its axis. I opened my mouth, then I shut it again. Being with Shuggie was like virtual reality or something. 'Who?'

'Orla,' he sighed, with a martyred air of patience.

'Why would I apologise to her? I haven't done anything!'

'Do you want to shag her or not?'

That did it. I swung round and grabbed his shoulders. I could feel my fingers sinking into his scrawny flesh and I knew I must be hurting him, but I couldn't think of anything to say to that reproachful, glassy gaze.

'Look, Nick, you're not gay or something, are you? Because I don't fancy you.'

He blinked up at me nervously, while my grip and my jaw went slack even as I wondered how to disembowel him without attracting attention. I suppose nervous blinking was Shuggie's incredibly clever defence mechanism. I was never going to beat him to death. So I let go of him and put my face in my hands to hide my laughter.

'Shugs, I swear –'

'Frequently. Look, it doesn't matter what you've done or haven't done. Orla's hard as nine-inch nails. You think anybody ever told her they're sorry about . . . um . . . you know? Nobody would dare bring up . . . you know. Nobody would mention it. She needs somebody to say sorry. She needs to talk about it. And if it's *you*, well . . . she'll be so shocked and grateful, she'll forget to think you're a dick.'

I clenched my loose jaw in case I started dribbling. What he said made a certain insane sense. Or maybe that was me clutching at straws. 'Is the atmosphere thin?'

'Where?'

'Up there on Planet Shuggie.'

He sighed and hitched his bag on to his shoulder. 'No one can help a man who doesn't want to be helped.'

'You're mad,' I said.

'Whatever you say.'

'Mad,' I said again.

'I have Physics now.' Dignified, he marched away.

'Heidcase!' I shouted after him. 'Feckin' heidcase! Think I'm stupit enough to take advice like that?'

6

Orla was in exactly the same position the following day at lunchtime. There were three things about this that bugged me. How did she get away with it, climbing over the fence in full view of McCluskey's office and sitting by the burn all lunchtime? And how come she'd shed her gang like a snakeskin in the last few days? And how was that a different book already? She'd obviously finished Albert Whatsisface because she was on to Ian McEwan, and as far as I knew this one wasn't a set book either.

'I'm sorry,' I mumbled to the back of her head.

Her right hand rested on Ian McEwan's pages. Gracefully, she lifted it and made it into a casual fist. Her middle finger uncurled, lingering in mid-air. I watched, fascinated by its gleaming black fingernail, as it lowered unhurriedly to turn another page.

Shuggie, I thought, you pointless wee waste of space,

thought and time.

But I was here now. Turning and walking away would be my ultimate loss of dignity and I would never recover from it. So I sat down at her side.

She didn't spare me a glance. At least I don't think she did, though it was hard to tell behind that gleaming, thick dark hair and the silver-blonde forelock that curved down across her face. I was sitting there as stiff and aggressive as a deep-frozen Dobermann, so I leaned casually back on one elbow and made all my muscles slouch. This position was incredibly uncomfortable, but I couldn't recover; I'd just have to let my spine sag and endure it. My jaw moved round some imaginary gum; then I stopped that, realising how stupid it looked.

'For God's sake,' sighed Orla. 'Sit up before you get cramp.'

I paused a moment, for dignity, then did as she said. I put my arms round my knees to stop myself putting them round her.

'I'm sorry about Allie,' I blurted. 'That's all. The way she's going on about Aidan and all. That's all I was going to say and I'd better go and –'

'Shut up,' said Orla, and turned another page.

'OK,' I said, swallowing. Never, I thought, never, never, never take Shuggie's ridiculous ideas seriously. Ever again.

'I don't want your stupid apology.'

'Right,' I said. 'Right. OK. I realise that. Sor . . . OK.'

I was waiting for her to tell me to eff off. I knew she would, eventually, and that I ought to leave before that final indignity, but I couldn't bring myself to stand up and walk away. Sitting there watching her half-hidden profile, I wasn't sure I actually liked Orla Mahon. Maybe it was because I felt guilty about her brother. Guilt, what a weird thing it is. I felt bad for her, so I disliked her.

I still wanted to sit next to her till it wasn't possible any more. Till the world fell into the sun, if she'd let me.

Neatly she folded down a triangle of page and closed her book, then laid it on the sparse grass beside her. Here it comes, I thought, a huge regretful ache clenching my guts.

Sitting forward she put her arms round her knees, the same position as me. That was a good sign, I thought, hope leaping crazily in my heart again. Call it a mood swing, but that was good, wasn't it? Mirroring your body language. Hadn't I read that somewhere?

Ah, hormones and lust: there's no reasoning with them.

'That was his name,' she said. 'Aidan.'

I chewed the inside of my cheek. Her voice was dry and bitter and cool and I didn't know quite where she was going with this, so I thought I'd keep my mouth shut.

'You said it,' she said. 'Aidan, you said it. Nobody's said his name to me in a whole year. Not outside my house.'

'Oh,' I said.

Wildly articulate. Oh, well done, Nicholas.

'You know the thing about your sister?' she said.

'Um . . .' I began. And stopped, because once more I didn't know where this was going.

'She's never stopped mentioning him,' said Orla.

'She never shuts up about him,' I pointed out, then wished I hadn't.

'True. But at least she talks about him. She doesn't pretend he never existed, y'know? She just pretends he still does. Which I think. You know. I like that better.'

We sat in silence. Weak sunlight prised through the branches and glanced off the burn's surface, making it gleam like an oily blade. I chucked in a dirty twig and watched it drift towards the whalemouth, but it caught against the rusty grille, tangled in a bit of blue plastic.

'It's just Allie's way of handling it,' I said. 'See?'

Orla's shoulder moved very slightly. 'Having a go at her, that's Mum's way of handling it.'

'So you're not . . .'

'I'm not bothered,' said Orla. 'Mum just says I am, because she doesn't want to admit she's upset about it herself. And she doesn't want your mum to know Allie upsets her. She thinks that would upset your mum. See?'

I did, sort of. 'Your mum,' I said. 'She's very . . .'

'Yes,' said Orla. 'She is.'

I threw the burn another twig. This one it caught, swirling it away into the tunnel.

'Your pal,' she said. 'That Shuggie.'

'He's not my pal,' I growled. 'He's a tick I can't get rid of.'

'Of course. You saved Shuggie's life and now you're responsible for him. His existence is down to you, so you owe it to him to look after him.'

'Oh, aye?'

'Aye,' she mimicked. 'It's a tradition in more than one culture.'

How elegantly she patronised. She said 'culture' as if she was trying to teach me a foreign language.

I thought about it for a moment. 'Not that I saved his actual life or anything, but I'd have thought it'd be the other way round.'

'Yes, but it isn't.'

'Well. Ain't life strange.'

'Ain't it.'

I thought for a minute that Orla Mahon was taking the mickey out of me, and that made me wildly, irrationally happy.

'So. Shuggie was telling me stuff about you,' she said.

Oh, was he? 'Such as?'

'He says you're desperate to shag me.'

I glanced at my watch. It was twenty past one now. There was time. He'd be dead by quarter to two and I could still get my *Handmaid's Tale* essay in.

'You're not getting to, of course.' Orla examined a polished black fingernail, smoothing down a peeling edge. 'But you can take us out if you want.'

'Yeah?' *Who says I want to do that?* was on the tip of my tongue, but fortunately I wasn't stupid enough to say it. 'Do you want to go to a movie?'

'No,' she said.

'Oh. Fine.'

'I'll meet you in Beppe's tomorrow evening and you can buy me a coffee.'

Bugger. That meant I'd have to make intelligent conversation. What was wrong with a movie, for God's sake? I swallowed my deep sense of dread and said, 'OK.'

She stood up, tucked Ian McEwan under her armpit (lucky, lucky Ian), and glared at me. 'Seven o'clock. Don't be late.'

As if, I wanted to scream. 'OK.'

I gave her two minutes' head start, during which I bounced up and down on my heels and cackled silently, like a madman, at the burn. Then, as I followed her up the bank, I glanced up at the fence. Bespectacled eyes gazed at me through the wire. There was a Physics textbook clasped in Shuggie's arms, and an expression of intense scientific inquiry on his face, as if he'd mixed a couple of lethal chemicals and was waiting for the test tube to explode.

THEN

7

Allie had never lost that fey strangeness she'd had as a baby, that solemn indifference to reality. I knew very well that she'd be a target for bullies despite her connections to the underworld (me), and from the day she started at Craigmyle High I had every intention of keeping an eye on her.

Things never work out. I had my own priorities, and more importantly Kev's priorities, and I could hardly stalk my own little sister around the playground. I consoled myself with the knowledge that even Allie had to learn life's number one lesson: you have to look after yourself.

Anyway, she wouldn't let me look after her. I was no longer her big brother and guardian angel – good for lending Marvel comics, getting rid of the spooky dream-catchers Mum hung around Allie's bedroom, and creating showjumping courses in the back garden for nonexistent ponies. Her shock must have killed that brother, but that was fine: he'd only ever existed in her head.

The parents had had complaints about me, of course, but Allie had simply had no idea. I'd led a double life without knowing I was doing it, without realising how much Allie's starry adoration meant to me. I stayed out late with my mates, but I never came home off my face or reeking of drink. After all, Dad was a hell of a role model in that respect. Anyway, when your pals are lashed it's easy enough to fool them into thinking you're drinking just as much as they are, but that drink only makes you surlier and sarkier.

No secrets now, though. Allie was on to me. She never did mention Calum's beating; she never referred to it, not once. Whatever she'd wanted so much to show me, I never did see it. It was probably something she'd made or painted at school, that was all, so I don't know why it bothered me so much. Allie turned her huge dark eyes from me and pretended I didn't exist, either at school or at home. Guilty and resentful, I started ignoring her, too.

That's why her swashbuckling saviour was not me, but studious, handsome, noble, sporty, sucky-up, clever-dick Aidan Mahon.

The twat.

It should never have happened. It *would* never have happened if I'd been there in time. The bit I missed, I soon caught up with: one more thing Dad wasn't going to let me forget. His little goddess had been threatened, and Dad was as smitten as she was with the boy who rescued her.

Five hard-faced girls had cornered her at breaktime in her fourth week at school. They were after her lunch money, but what they were really hoping for was a fight. Her money clasped in her fist, Allie being Allie she hesitated, which was what they wanted. She was strange, she was silent, she stuck out: what she needed, clearly, was a good kicking.

I could have told her that, of course. I could have told her the facts of life if I'd been there, but I was on the other side of the science block when it started, and Kev was the one who told me what was going on, and he took his time about it.

'Did you not do something?' I bellowed.

'Nah,' said Kev, shrugging. 'Thought I'd tell you instead.'

It struck me that Kev didn't like Allie that much.

I was anxious, but it seemed important to look cool about this, so I didn't run. I walked fast, hands in pockets, panicking only a little. I knew she couldn't come to too much harm before I got there. They were novice neds, and too stupid to know when they'd picked the wrong target.

A small crowd was gathering: you can always spot a scrap by the audience. The five girls hadn't noticed me. They were chanting their loathing, and the first girl was swinging her bag at Allie's legs to tangle them and trip her, and I was thinking about starting to run, and wondering how that would look, when Aidan Mahon turned the corner.

He'd come upon them by accident, but he was a lot closer than I was. He was with some other handsome rugby-playing type (God, but they're irritating) but Aidan didn't even wait for his friend. Without so much as pausing for breath and a hasty risk-assessment, he waded in and ripped the bag from the little bitch's hands.

I came to a frozen halt. So what was the smooth thing to do in this unprecedented situation? She was my sister. I was too late. But I wasn't Aidan Mahon's sidekick and I didn't want to look like an afterthought.

My mind was such a chaos of shock I couldn't hear what Aidan said to the five girls. He had the advantage of surprise, of course, and he had Allie by the arm, and even I would have thought twice before tangling with somebody his size, even though he was a year younger than me. Whatever he snapped at them, it had an effect. They scowled, but they backed away pretty fast as he shoved past them, escorting Allie out of their circle. Humiliated, they slouched away, muttering. I don't think the wee gangsters even managed to swear at him, they were so stunned.

I hesitated. I should go up to her, I thought, and ask if she was OK. I should tell her I'd been on my way, she didn't have to worry, I wouldn't have let anything happen to her.

I'd have done all that if she'd looked at me once. She

didn't. She knew I was there, but she never even turned her head. She said something quietly to Aidan, and he smiled and flushed a little.

They walked within a few metres of me, but my sister still didn't look my way.

Allie was his shadow after that, and the annoying thing is, Aidan didn't seem to mind. He almost seemed to like her. Perhaps he was too tolerant and kind to tell her where to go.

The big frigging cowboy, what was he thinking of? He was two years older than her. He should have shrugged her off, told her he'd got her out of a tight spot but that didn't mean he wanted a stalker. No way should he have led my sister on. He should have treated her with amused condescension, accepted a certain degree of hero-worship but made it quite clear he didn't have a romantic interest.

That's how *I'd* have done it.

Aidan wasn't me, though. He wasn't anything like me. I wondered how his mind worked, and I developed a permanent sinking feeling.

You cannot cow little cows indefinitely, and it wasn't Allie's last brush with trouble. But that day her dark eyes grew shining stars in their depths that never went out again, ever glittering with the reflection of Aidan's glory. I had blown my chance to be my sister's hero but at least she'd found another one, and I hated and respected him for it.

Dad, of course, wouldn't hear a word against Aidan. One morning I tried to spin some negative propaganda in the shape of my suspicions about Aidan's intentions, but where Allie was concerned Dad had rose-tinted contact lenses (unless that was his morning-after eyeballs).

'Of course Aidan likes her,' he told me. 'Who wouldn't?' He was staring at his *Guardian*, badly folded with trembling hands, but I could tell he wasn't really reading it. He was too annoyed with me, and last night's empty bottle of red was parked beside the recycling bucket, and Lola Nan had been dawn-hoovering again.

'He's older than Allie,' I said, being skilled in Stating the Bleeding Obvious.

'So?'

I'd picked a bad time, but the phone had rung and Mum had disappeared to her under-stairs sanctum in a swish of skirt and hair and glitter. We were alone together unexpectedly. I said, 'Don't want Mahon to think he can take advantage of Allie just 'cause she's younger.'

'He's not like that. He's not that kind of boy.'

Not, in other words, *like you, Nick.* I could hear that one vibrating telepathically in the air.

'Anyhow,' I persisted, 'he just lets her hang on his coat-tails. Likes her trailing him like a puppy.' That wasn't quite how it was, and there wasn't any actual romance going on, but I was pissed off with Dad, with Aidan, with Allie. 'It's not like he ever takes her to films or anything. Not as if he makes any kind of an *effort*.'

Dad stood up sharply, almost unbalanced, and grabbed dirty breakfast dishes off the table while he got his equilibrium back.

'Make up your bloody mind, Nick,' he snapped.

Losing my temper, in a silent way, I walked out.

No change in that relationship then. Dad and I were not made for hearty man-to-man chats. Anyway, I'd already made up my mind.

I hated Aidan Mahon; I loved his big sister. I'd fallen like a stone, smitten, the day she watched me beat the crap out of Calum, the day she decided I was scum. That timing was bad enough.

But I loved her from the moment I saw her grab Kev's nuts and twist so hard she nearly had them off.

8

I remember the day Kev decided to have a go at Aidan. I remember very well that it was only a week after he tried it on with Orla – which was when she let him know, in words of no syllables at all, what she thought of that idea. Kev had screamed with flabbergasted pain and Sunil and I thought our heads were going to explode with the pressure of not laughing.

Orla had humiliated Kev big time, but Kev could hardly take it out on Orla, since Orla was tougher and harder than he was and there would be hell to pay later. Her brother Aidan, similarly aloof but a year younger and less well-connected, would have to pay for Kev's bruised genitals and his almost mortally wounded pride.

Less well-connected, my arse. All I'm doing is making excuses for myself. Aidan was perfectly popular and belonged to several clubs and got on fine with everybody in them. All I'm saying in a mealy craven way is he didn't have a gang.

Perhaps I mean 'less smart'. Or 'less feral'. Or 'not entirely familiar with the facts of life'. He was not, however, daft enough to argue with Kev.

That day Allie was hanging out with him as usual. I don't know what I'd expected: perhaps that Aidan had finally remembered she was two years younger, had done the decent thing and told her where to go. Or perhaps, miraculously, Allie would have fallen out of love, lust and hero-worship, found a new friend and forgotten Aidan.

The gods had not had a change of heart.

Still, I told myself, it would be good for Allie to see that her hero had feet of clay, that he wasn't Superman, he wasn't even Clark Kent. Maybe I thought she'd find new respect for me, that she'd notice Aidan wasn't the alpha male around here: I was.

What bizarre thought process convinced me that because I was only Kev's protector, because I'd shackled myself to him out of pity, self-preservation and respect for his brother, that I was somehow better than him? It was one of those subjective-viewpoint things. Kev was a gangster, Sunil was a henchman, I was a noble savage. Kev was a brutal dictator, Sunil was a thug, I was a foot-soldier.

I did not think things through.

I have to admit it: they were sweet together, Aidan and

Allie. My sister was not good at making friends, and when she did it was with other quiet studious girls who were no threat to her self-possession but would be no earthly use in a crisis either. None of them were going to turn into lifelong pals, but you could sort of tell that Aidan might. He treated her like an equal, age-wise. He consoled her when other harder girls got their barbs in. He told her bad jokes, warned her about teachers' foibles, helped her with her homework, covered for her when she needed covering. He looked out for her. Which was supposed to be my job.

I was more like my dad than I'd ever wanted to be. I was like a drinker who couldn't drag himself back to fresh air till he'd sunk to his lowest ebb. Like Dad was never going to do.

Aidan was not exactly a soft target but there were enough of us. He was on his own that day, except for Allie, penned with him in the malevolent half-noose of boys. She wasn't in the line of fire, of course: Kev knew better in those days than to have a go at my sister, but she was pressed against the fence behind her hero. Now that I think about it, Aidan had shoved her back there, shoved her back and stepped in front of her and glared at me with all the contempt in the world. Cutting his eyes away, he looked at Kev Naughton.

'Go and give us your phone, then,' sneered Kev.

I sneered too, till my eyes met Allie's.

She didn't look hurt at all, not even shocked, just

reproachful. As if she knew fine it was myself I was hurting; I wasn't capable of hurting her. That I was just capable of better. *You're a disappointment to me, Nick*, that's the message I got loud and clear.

My heart tore with the shame of it. My lowest ebb. About time too.

Shaking his head, Aidan smiled at Kev. 'Won't your mum buy you one? Here you go. Happy Christmas.' And he tossed the phone to Kev.

Kev could have let it drop to the ground, but by reflex he caught it. Somehow that made it even more humiliating: taking catches for Aidan. It was a prize, that phone. Slim as a blade, matt black, state of the art. And Aidan tossed it to Kev like a trifle, like Kev was a charity case who needed it more than he did.

When Aidan turned on his heel and walked towards me, I stepped out of his way without thinking. For that I got a killing glare from Sunil, but I couldn't retrieve the situation without making the lot of us look even stupider. Besides, Allie was marching after Aidan and no way was I getting in her way. She took no notice of me as she barged past.

Funnily enough, I didn't feel too bad. Aidan had made Kev look a fool, and I realised I was not unhappy about that. In fact, I got a keen sneaky pleasure from it.

A switch tripped in my brain. I felt like I'd caught sight of a small circle of sky above a stinking pit, one I'd climbed in all by myself. Now I could start to claw my way back up to the human race because I didn't feel like the worst scum on the planet any more; maybe just the second- or third-worst scum. I knew Allie and I would be fine in the end.

I'd have been entirely content with the way the mugging turned out if I hadn't been so afraid for Aidan. And I am right about some things, because very shortly afterwards I betrayed Kev to save Shuggie Middleton's backside, and Mister Hero saw me do it, and was inspired to more and greater and stupider acts of heroism, and died of it.

9

Shuggie Middleton. His Adam's apple bobbled and jerked as I glared into his blankly intelligent eyes. Oh, the fickleness of natural selection. Why were the smart ones always at the bottom of the food chain? What did it benefit the human race that the likes of Kev and Mickey Naughton were the ultimate predators? Ah well. No accounting for evolution. Back to the matter in hand.

Shuggie's eyes for once were not screened by his glasses, as those were lying on the tarmac stomped into shards under Kev Naughton's boot. He wouldn't hand over his lunch money and he didn't have a phone to hand over, which was another bad move, because it just made Kev irrationally angry. If I'd been Shuggie, I'd have got my mum to buy me a cheap one for a sacrificial offering. But I was smarter than Shuggie. In some ways I was.

I'd been uneasy about targeting the wee oddball from

the start. I felt sorry for him since he'd lost his dad, who I used to see a lot when Allie and Shuggie were at primary and she was always round at his house. When I went round there to drag Allie away for her tea, I used to be scared of his father's height and presence and his fierce searching eyes. In the end the fear was diluted with a juvenile unthinking pity, but it never went away altogether.

Shuggie's dad was a mathematician. I think that's what he was, anyway. I'm not sure what a mathematician does in real life (as my former Maths teacher will confirm) so maybe he was a professor of mathematics or something. At any rate, I can't say he used to be a mathematician before he got sick because he didn't *used to be* anything, even then. It wasn't his brain that stopped working, just his fingers. At first. Then, gradually, so did everything else: legs, arms, neck, the lot, right down to his tongue and his throat.

But his brain never did stop working; it wasn't like Lola Nan. He went on being a mathematician, but a furious one. Shuggie's dad's eyes were diamond clear and diamond hard and full of rage, even as his body curled in on itself and wasted into a rickle of sticks and his head sagged forward in its brace. He could still force his eyeballs up to glare at you, intelligence blazing out of them along with a lasering anger. Whatever he had it felled him like a tree, only he took a terribly long time to fall: slow motion that lasted about a year. Since he couldn't swallow or speak, he choked to death one day on his own spit, which seemed like a fittingly angry death.

If Shuggie had inherited just half his dad's ferocity he'd never have been a target for Kev, but here we were, and there he was, and I'd been outvoted. And his glasses were destroyed and that was going to cost his mother a good bit more than a phone or some lunch money. I remember wanting to grab the child by the scruff of the neck, drag him into a corner and explain that to him in words of one syllable. A black wriggling worm of guilt had lodged in my gut a little over a week ago, but I'd done nothing about it. I remembered Allie's cold contempt, and Aidan's piss-taking bravado, and I tried to remember that feeling of crashing to the bottom of the pit and rolling over to see the sky a million miles overhead. I tried to remember how I'd planned to reach it.

Instead I stood there like the expendable henchman I was, giving Shuggie the empty-eyed stare that usually got them turning out their pockets for Kev. It wasn't working, and I could feel the atmosphere worsening in our dingy corner. I did not like the shuffling impatience of the others, the charge of eager aggression in the air. I did not like the wolfpack scent of us. I knew Kev had an unreasonable and chippy pride, sharpened by the humiliations of Orla and Aidan, and I did not like the idea of what he might do to salvage it.

What I did like was the stupid defiance in Shuggie's myopic gaze. He just stood there with his hands curled into tight fists, arms poker-straight at his sides. He looked at me – roughly, I mean we're talking Blind Pew here – and he looked at Sunil, big and threatening on Kev's left hand, and then he looked at Kev. His lower lip was stuck out, his spotty chin tilted half-heartedly, as if he'd committed himself to resistance without really thinking it through, but he knew he might as well take what was coming because there was no getting out of it now. Up against the seven of Kev's regulars he looked brave and stoical and entirely defenceless.

Kev crunched his knuckles, having seen too many cheap Cockney gangster films, and just then I knew I couldn't bear it. I couldn't bear what was going to happen to Shuggie, right under my eyes. I couldn't bear to be part of it. Mostly, and quite suddenly, I couldn't bear being on the same planet as Kev Naughton.

'Leave him alone,' I said.

It just did not compute in Kev's brain for a while, and for that I don't blame him. He didn't know who the hell I was talking to, he didn't know why I'd blurted that out like some badly programmed Terminator, he didn't understand. He smirked at Shuggie for a few seconds longer, his brow furrowing gradually till the smirk faded to a perplexed frown.

'Leave him,' I said again. I'd started now and I couldn't unsay it, so I'd better follow this through or I'd had it. 'Leave him alone, Kev.'

Kev turned and stared at me. There was confusion in

his eyes, and betrayal, and a degree of hurt, but even as I watched, it all coalesced into sheer contempt. That was it. It was irreversible, and I knew I'd burned my boats with a few impetuous words and a moment of misplaced sympathy. Oh, feck.

I could feel the combined stare of all of them, including Shuggie, but I wasn't wasting my energy looking anywhere but at Kev. I was the biggest and the meanest of them and they'd certainly take me down and give me a hiding if they got up the nerve and moved as one, but nobody wanted to suffer for making the first move. Anyway, they were all trying to get their heads round what had changed. Some of them weren't that bright, though you couldn't say that of Kev (though I only discovered much later, in a courtroom, just how smart he was).

'Why don't you piss off and play with the girls, Nick?' he sneered, half turning back to Shuggie.

'Cause they're harder than you,' I said, 'and I'm dead scared of them.'

I heard a couple of muffled snorts, turning quickly to coughs, and knew I was maybe OK with a few of them – they wouldn't hit me too hard, they'd only pretend. That still left Sunil, though, and a couple of others, and Kev.

'Leave the wee tosser alone,' I said.

'You gonnae make me do that?'

'Uh-huh. Yeah, Kev. I'm gonnae.' There was a small Nick inside my skull at that moment, headbutting my brain and shouting at me to shut *up*, but really I didn't have a choice now. I had to bluff my way out or I really was screwed. 'Just leave him, OK?' I was not getting any more original with my pleas, but I was reckoning, Keep It Simple, Stupid. Because by that time, I was feeling extremely stupid.

'You.' I looked at Shuggie, and jerked my head. 'Eff off out of here.'

Shuggie was not as dumb as I was. He didn't hang around hoping to protect *me*. He just effed off out of there.

For the moment, as it turned out, I didn't need protecting. Kev was so stunned by my betrayal he just stood and stared as I walked past him, but it was not a nice stare. I know that because I held his eyes as long as I could. The others weren't going to do anything without his say-so, not now. Later.

It was as I shoved past the last of them that I spotted Aidan. He'd been walking round the corner on the way to the maths annexe, which was a grand title for a couple of prefab huts. He was standing rock-still, as if he'd watched everything, and he was staring at me, his eyes beneath their fair fringe brilliant with shocked approval, which made me want to hit him.

This was not long before he became imaginary.

NOW

10

'They're trying to kill me,' whispered Lola Nan. 'They've paid a hitman and I never know which moment could be my last.'

Mum was fighting a jar of organic fairtrade marmalade, trying to get the lid off. Dad sat at the table watching her, jaw in his fists, faded tattoos wrinkled and crumpled, wispy hair coming out of its elastic band. He gave Lola Nan a filthy look.

'Why would we go to the expense when we could shove you under a bus?'

'Terence!' said Mum.

I'd sooner push you under one, I thought, than ever do it to Lola Nan. But Dad caught my eye and tried to give me a knowing smile, like it was a shared joke. Pathetic.

Poor Dad. We'd lost contact in his smitten love affair with Allie. Now he knew she was going to grow up too, whether he liked it or not, and maybe he'd like to be in touch with me again, but he didn't know where to start. Neither did I, so we were on a bit of a hiding to nothing.

Sometimes I got the notion he was thinking about not having the first drink of the evening, so that he wouldn't be dazed, and he'd remember to sit down with me and talk, clear-headed meaningful bonding stuff. Then he'd think about not having the second drink instead, but he'd have it anyway, and a third. After that he'd be dazed and the bonding thing wouldn't seem so important any more.

'Nick,' said Mum.

I dreaded that bright and brittle tone. Hesitant, afraid to begin. 'What?' I said.

'Did you hear Kevin Naughton's mother died?'

I had to take a quick breath. 'No,' I said calmly. 'When?'

'Last week? Sometime last week.' She banged the marmalade jar hard a few times on the table. I don't know what that was supposed to achieve. 'It was in the weekend paper.'

'Oh,' I said. 'You didn't show me.'

'I wasn't sure . . . I didn't know if you'd . . .'

Didn't think I'd care, eh? 'Was it the cancer?' I asked.

Mum nodded, straining at the jar lid. I wished Dad would get his finger out and give her a hand. I wished Mum would snap at him, tell him to stop being such an idle troll. 'She had a recurrence,' she said. 'It came back with a vengeance. Jenna Mathieson from the oncology ward told me. So sad.'

So sad.

Came back with a vengeance.

Shame, it really was. Poor woman. Her parenting skills might have been dodgy, or they might not, but *she* never killed anyone. A shiver rippled down my spine. 'Maybe it was Kev's trial,' I said. 'Stress.'

'Don't talk crap,' snapped Dad. 'The woman had cancer. That can be fatal, you know.'

Sarcastic *arse*.

Mum gave him that look she always did: surprised, and slightly sympathetic. I don't know why she should be surprised. It wasn't exactly out-of-character behaviour. Must have been a rough night. Again.

Sure enough, 'I need a drink,' he muttered under his breath.

I knew he wouldn't have one. Drinking after breakfast would make him an alcoholic. He said it for my benefit, just to let me know how much I upset him. So damn disappointed in me, he was driven to drink. Poor little arse.

Lola Nan threw me one of her rare incisive glances, though it landed just over my left shoulder. 'Me too.' She flashed a wicked grin. 'Any whisky?'

Most of the time I knew Lola Nan was gone. But there were times I suspected a lucid old gremlin hid behind her papery eyelids.

'Later, Lola Nan.' I patted the fragile hand that in turn was patting its little cushion of air. 'I have to go to *school* now.'

Focusing, she snatched her hand away. 'Wasn't talking to you!' she screamed.

Great. My last contact with the human race didn't remember who I was. I didn't know my father, my mother was too embarrassing to know, my sister was psychologically unhinged and on top of everything else I was Billy Nae-Pals and had been for more than a year now.

This might have been partly my own fault, since very few people extended the hand of friendship in case it got bitten off. I'd put a lot of energy into my public image. Boy, was it paying off.

From my old gang, Kev's friends, I was ostracised, excommunicated. I was as dazed as Dad on a Friday night, but with an unfocused anger and a sense of violent injustice. Funny how I was the great untouchable, when it was Kev who'd . . .

Well, there was no way back with Kev, which was lucky because I didn't want one. Shuggie was not much of a replacement gang, but for once I felt extremely benevolent towards him. The lights had come on in my head, so dazzling I couldn't sleep for the glare. To hell with Dad; to hell with ex-friends and imaginary ones. I had a date with Orla Mahon. Tonight.

A worm of unease had been nibbling at my guts, but I put that down to excitement – anticipation, nerves, lust, whatever. I wasn't letting myself associate it with the sniggers of Orla's posse yesterday afternoon. Anyway, she'd shut them up fast enough. All but Gina, who was a hard girl to shut up, but she'd choked and spluttered so long into her Tango, Orla had finally sworn at her and kicked her ankle.

I'd had to turn away to hide my stupid smile. Orla Mahon, no less, was sticking up for *me*. No need for the squirming ball of nerves in my gut then. No reason to let it distract me.

It did though. Between nerves and ecstasy, I wasn't capable of thinking about anything else. That must be why, when I pulled the front door shut behind me and jogged down the concrete path that morning, I had my hand on the rusty iron gate before I recognised the car parked across the road.

Dark blue Mondeo. Fancy rims. A suit jacket hung carefully in the back. Tinted windows, but the driver's side was down and a lean, muscled arm rested on the sill, crisp shirt sleeve rolled neatly to the elbow. Lola Nan's hitman, eh? Easy mistake to make, even with a functioning brain. After all, the nearest sexually challenged cow was some way from our street, so what was *he* doing here?

I stopped, not breathing, my hand tightening on the gate till flakes of rusty metal dug into my palm. He didn't worry me. He didn't scare me, I told myself. When a few repetitions of that didn't convince me, I tried to picture him at his day job. Mickey Naughton, up to his armpit in a startled Fricsian. Dreamy look in his eyes.

Still didn't work.

I tried to focus on his shadowy face. He was looking right at me, an unpleasant sneer on the side of his mouth. Mickey had a thin face, a handsome face, and Kev's girlfriend had once assured me those shadowy eyes were sexy. Dangerously so.

Kevin Naughton's mother died. Did you hear?

She had cancer. That can be fatal, you know.

That can be fatal.

Stupidhead.

Mickey lifted his fist like a wee boy pretending to have a gun, his first and second fingers jutting out to make the barrel. He pointed it not at me, but at the upstairs window of our house. He was aiming at the parents' room, had he but known it, but I wasn't tempted to laugh at his mistake.

Came back with a vengeance.

His finger gun jerked up with the imagined recoil, then he brought it to his lips and blew away imaginary smoke. Mickey smiled at me.

He didn't do anything as cheaply dramatic as screeching away. He turned the key lazily in the ignition, nosed the car into the road and drove out of sight.

THEN

11

Aidan was exactly the wrong age to witness my wee Clint Eastwood performance with Shuggie. He was fifteen, just one year younger than me: young enough to be reckless, old enough to be brave.

Never do heroics. Even if they do you no harm yourself, some stupid shining-eyed tosser will be far too impressed. And then a few months later they'll try to live up to your pointless example, and that's when they'll get themselves killed.

I got my overdue kicking a week after my defection. They were waiting for me to drop my guard, which I didn't, but I thought I'd probably better get it over with. I'd been the other end of the boot myself, so there was no point making an official complaint.

They were waiting among the sick-looking trees on

that footpath beside the computer store, and I was expecting them. It was only about half the crew, four or five of them. Nice to know I was popular. It didn't take long because only Kev's heart was really in it – honestly, I was quite touched.

This didn't mean they didn't put the boot in quite efficiently, of course, because a kicking's a kicking. Eventually, I hoped, some teacher pulling out of the school gates in his car would decide he couldn't in all conscience drive on by, even when it was only me.

You don't fight back. Everybody says that. And you know what? They're right. I just curled in on myself, since the most important thing was to protect my head and my guts, not to mention my precious genitals. For the most part I managed to achieve all this, but you can't protect everything all at once. So that's when my nose got broken.

The teacher with the conscience, luckily, was McCluskey. When his car turned out of the gates, he swerved on to the kerb, leaping out practically before he'd braked, purple with fury. Obviously he couldn't touch anyone for fear of being sued, but they legged it anyway, because nobody ever liked to push McCluskey to the point where they – or their bereaved parents – might be forced to sue him. He had a natural moral authority; in other words, he scared the living shit out of everybody.

Risking a timeout for a second, Sunil bent down to me. 'Sorry 'bout that,' he muttered, then hared away with the rest of them.

Dragging me up by the arm, McCluskey laid into me like it was my fault, which in a way it was.

'You stupid wee fecker, Geddes.' He could shout like this because he was outside the gates and outside school hours, or at least that's what I assumed. Whatever, I wasn't going to upbraid him for his language. 'You thick tossers want to kill each other, just do it when I'm not going to fall over your bleeding corpses. Right?'

'Right, sir,' I mumbled through a mouthful of blood and a nose that didn't belong to me. The words I managed to get out, I won't even try to spell phonetically. 'Understood.'

'What are you, Geddes?'

'Stupid fecker, sir.'

'Stupid *wee* fecker, and . . . ?'

'Stupid wee fecker and a thick tosser. *Sir.*'

He sighed and stared at my face, gripping my arm too hard because I was swaying. I didn't like to wipe my nose in case it looked like I was snivelling, which was some-thing McCluskey would not tolerate, but there was a warm stream of blood coming out of both nostrils, and McCluskey briefly let me go, fumbled in his car and shoved a faceful of tissues on to my nose. He caught me in the nick of time, just as I was about to lose my centre of gravity all over again.

'Are you all right, Geddes?'

'Uh-huh.'

'Aye, right.' He sighed. 'Look, Nick. You're smart and you're not a bad guy. Right?'

'Aye, right,' I mimicked.

His face darkened again. 'That's not smart. That's stupid. Stop trying to be stupider than you are, Geddes.'

'Right, sir.' He had the knack of making me feel ashamed of myself, and what was with all the flaming 'sirs'? McCluskey made me feel like I was in the army or something.

'It may be cool to be stupid, Geddes, but it is phenomenally stupid to want nothing more than to be cool. Why in God's name did you ever get involved with a loser like Naughton?'

I gave him my stupid-question-sir look.

He held on to his temper. 'Can I give you a lift home?'

'You are fecking joking, aren't you?' I said. 'Sir.'

Instant death sentence for fraternising with enemy aliens, and he knew it. 'I suppose I am, Geddes, I suppose I am. Are you sure you're all right? Well, even if you aren't, I suppose there's nothing I can do about it. What are your parents going to say about this?'

'I'll deal with them, sir.'

'I see.' Experimentally he let go of my arm, and I managed not to fall over.

'I won't be pressing charges, sir.'

'Funny ha ha.' He gave me a last sharp look. 'I heard about Hugh Middleton, by the way. You're improving.'

For a moment I didn't have a blind clue what he was on

about. 'Oh. Shuggie.'

'Geddes, it's just as well you're a big ugly thug who's perfectly capable of looking after yourself. Otherwise I'd be worried about you.'

'But I am a big ugly thug, sir,' I pointed out. 'So don't let me keep you awake nights.'

'You don't.' He got into his car, wound down the window and chucked me another handful of tissues. When I dropped the blood-soaked batch in the gutter, he didn't tick me off. 'If your parents want to make a complaint ask them to contact me.'

That was pure officialese and he knew it. Just as my bravado was all spit and wind, and I knew it. My nose was bleeding so much I thought I was going to bleed to death (I know better now what that actually looks like) so when he'd gone I staggered back to the deserted school and through the swing doors into the toilets and propped myself over a basin to watch my blood swirl away. I blinked really hard and tried not to fall over.

'The state of you,' said a voice behind me.

By now I couldn't help going abusive. 'Puck off,' I said. 'Pucked up by ettire life, you.'

Undeterred, Shuggie soaked some loo roll and started cleaning up my face, not seeming to consider the notion that I might feel like breaking *his* nose. I didn't, though, because the cold water felt good: soothing, numbing, as if it was soaking through my skin and all the way into my brain. I was terribly tired anyway and I could almost have fallen asleep on my feet, but just as my eyelids sagged, Shuggie coughed and stepped back to examine his handi-work. Nodding contentedly, he flushed away the bloody paper, and I muttered 'Danks.'

'Thank *you*, Nicholas,' he said.

'Puck off, Thuggie,' I said.

'You don't mean that.'

'Buddy do.'

'Well, I understand. But thank you anyway.' His gaze was very direct and unswerving. 'You know, we have to look after each other now. I have to look after you. And you have to look after me.'

'Like buddy hell I do!'

'Of course you do. You haven't got any friends left.'

'Danks a buddy punch.'

He shrugged. 'You're welcome. It was very brave of you.'

'Bave,' I glowered. 'As in toopid.'

'Bave,' he said, 'as in bave.'

His solemn straight face quivered not a jot so I had no excuse to hit him, though I knew fine Shuggie was laughing at me. Silently. Like an emotionally incontinent drain.

Shuggie Middleton was laughing at *me*.

If I thought Shuggie had got me looking remotely respectable, I was kidding myself. Distorted body image or something, looking at my reflection in the striplit toilet mirrors and thinking the black eye and the skinned cheekbone and the swollen jaw didn't look too bad, and that I could walk without almost doubling up. When I got home and Mum dropped her mug of tea, I just said 'Football.'

'Nick!' She half crouched, not knowing whether to start with me or the broken mug and the spilt tea.

'Rough tackle.'

Standing up straight, she bit her lip hard and I saw tears blur her green mascara. She wanted to hug me, that was obvious, but I hunched my shoulders and turned as if to leave the room. Clenching her hands at her sides, she blinked. 'It's not games day, Nick.'

Hmm. More switched on than I thought.

'What happened to you, Nick?'

'Told you. Bad foul.'

'No, Nick.' She had her hands full of broken china and I saw she'd cut the base of her thumb. She glanced down at the welling blood and she just let the drops spill darkly on to the carpet as she looked back up at me with tears burning in her green-rimmed eyes. 'No. I mean, what happened to you?'

I just looked at her. I don't think I've ever been so angry in my life. Part of me wanted to take the china shards out of her cupped hands and take her thumb and kiss the blood off it. The other half of me wanted to hit her.

'You wouldn't know,' I said. 'You were busy.'

'You never tell me anything!'

'You were busy,' I said again. 'What was I supposed to do?'

It sounded like cheek. But the fact is, I really wanted her to tell me.

'You were supposed to come to me.' But she sounded only sad.

'It's too late now.' That was the arrogance of youth speaking. Like I knew everything. Like everything that could ever happen to me had already happened. Hah.

'It is not too late! I'm going to see Mr Pearson and . . .' Her voice died under my glare.

I had to explain to her, in words of one syllable, that if she went anywhere near the Brain I'd make it clear it was all my fault, I started it, I was to blame. I was, after all, to blame. So in the end all Mum could do was drag me to A & E, where a doctor gave me a disapproving glare as she checked me over and sucked her teeth and stuck a dressing over my nose.

'Suits you,' said the woman tartly, eyeing her handiwork.

But that was all she said. She was busy with the deserving poorly and didn't want to know anything about my little fracas. Anyway, she thought she already knew everything.

In school assembly next day we got the obligatory pained lecture on the futility of violence. This was not McCluskey's idea, though undoubtedly it was his fault, since he must have felt obliged to report the incident to Pearson. It was a wildly irrelevant lecture, given that anyone in your average secondary school knows that violence is anything but futile, but Pearson liked to give it to us now and then, maybe so he could meet his anti-bullying targets. (There was no bullying culture at Craigmyle High. The Brain knew this because back when there was a bullying culture, he'd had the bright idea of getting bullies into dialogue with their victims. The programme was a huge success: after not very long, victims stopped turning up, since the perpetrators never failed to. These occasions were great for looking contrite, sounding sorry, and finding out what was really, really working on the bullying front.)

McCluskey sat on the head's left, arms folded, glowering into the middle distance, meeting no one's eyes and certainly not mine. What his body language said was this: *I know the guy on my right is a prat. I know you have no respect for him. But until he shuts up and lets us all get on with our respective jobs, I will personally kill any giggler.* It was like watching some politician give a speech to squaddies. The regimental sergeant major was up there next to the defence minister, and the squaddies knew if they stepped out of line they were going to die.

So we were all remarkably good in the circumstances. As usual somebody off to my left was quietly humming the theme tune to *Pinky and the Brain*, and others were harmonising, and this was making some first years practically explode into fragments with the effort of not laughing, which was of course the whole point. I wanted to start singing 'Imagine', which would have got me all kinds of complex Brownie points in my school rehabilitation, because it would be taking the mickey out of my notorious mother as well as our intense and well-meaning head. But I ached all over, my ribs and my nose hurt too much and any tune would have been unrecognisable. Besides, I found I couldn't quite do that to my mother, even if I'd happily do it to Pearson.

Anyway, though McCluskey was ignoring the music merchant, his super-senses would lock on to me straight away. I was disgusted to discover that I cared what McCluskey thought of me and I didn't want him to go on thinking I was stupid.

I certainly wasn't the sharpest lemon in the bag. This is when I pocketed one of Mum's kitchen knives and started carrying it to school.

12

In the last couple of months of his final term, not having my feelings to consider any more, Kev did his best to make up for lost opportunities where my sister was concerned. It was the same as with Orla: he was scared of her, so he targeted Aidan. He was scared of me (still), so he targeted Allie. And the big shining best of it, from Kev's point of view, was that Allie was not just a way of getting at me: she was also a way of getting at Aidan.

Killing two birds, that's what they call it.

There were still constraints on him: namely, the Despot McCluskey, and the fact that I could still kill the wee tosser with my bare hands if he went too far.

So what he did was he got the girls to do it for him. This meant I was worse than useless. Girls outclass boys a hundred times over when it comes to making someone's life a misery, especially when it's another girl. Allie was persecuted in the toilets, in the PE changing rooms, any-where they could get her alone.

It was not that easy to provoke Allie to tears but they managed it quite often. Shuggie would come to get me, but by the time I raced to her aid she'd be standing quietly as Aidan talked to her (the first time), or sitting against the fence with him, their shoulders pressed together (the second time). On various occasions after that, I watched him wipe her face dry with the palm of his hand. I watched him put an arm round her shoulders. A few days later I watched her press her face into his neck and I think she kissed him because his face reddened and his throat jerked with his gulp. Next time I saw his lips touch hers experimentally. After that it all went beyond experiment.

So he was finally making an effort. Finally taking advantage. The *tosser*.

From then on he'd hold Allie's hand, but only when he thought I wasn't around. Was he scared of me, or was the big cowboy considering my feelings?

Didn't matter. When I was around and he did not take her hand, she would ostentatiously take his.

By the first week of the next school year, Aidan and Allie were firmly and finally an item. I seethed. The age gap! But I looked at her and realised over the summer she'd stopped being my strange little sister. She was starting to be beautiful in a grown-up sort of way. And how could I say anything anyway? He was there for her when I wasn't.

It was Aidan she went to, always Aidan.

It was four months since the incident with Shuggie, four months since I burned my boats with Kev. Allie was just into her second year, Aidan his fourth, and I'd stayed, to McCluskey's horror, for a fifth.

'Geddes,' he greeted me as I sloped in on my first morning. 'Oh, the joy of it.'

'I'm touched, Mr McCluskey. It's nice to see you too.'

He clasped his hands and closed his eyes. 'Dear God. What did I do in a past life?'

'Were you some kind of evil fascist dictator, sir?'

'Aye, and I shot the likes of you for sport before breakfast. Get lost, Geddes.'

'I missed you too, sir.'

The way his scowl was working and twitching, he was either livid with rage or he was trying not to smile. I couldn't quite tell as I slouched off in the direction of the science block.

I'd been afraid I might hate being in school when I didn't have to be, but what happened was quite the reverse. The atmosphere without Kev was different. The worst of his gang had gone with him, and the ones who stayed, like Sunil, discovered they didn't have quite the same aura of menace without him and anyway to a large extent they'd lost interest. Maybe we'd just started to grow up. I was still Billy Nae-Pals, but English and my Science subjects were shaping up to be kind of interesting and the teachers treated me with – well, not exactly affection, but at least a bit more respect. I was there from choice and once they got over their shock they seemed to appreciate that. I think things might have turned right around if Kev hadn't still been haunting the place.

I reckon he was missing school a bit, missing his easy work-free life and his status as large shark sniffing round the blood trails in a smallish pond. Partly, of course, he was showing off: his souped-up car, his manky big-label fashion choices, his superior wee I'm-a-grown-up sneer.

McCluskey got bored of telling Kev to go away (though not in those words), but there was a limit to what he could do about it. He couldn't prove Kev was flogging cannabis to first years, though I knew fine he was. I think, given time, McCluskey would have got the better of Kev, but he never did get time. None of us did. Aidan Mahon's time, of course, ran out altogether.

Allie should have come to me. She should have come to *me*, but she never did. That's why I'm alive and Aidan isn't.

13

I think it started out like any other day. I suppose they always do. The sky wasn't a cloudless blue, but nor was there a louring, ominous darkness. There were clouds from horizon to horizon, halfway up the sky and uninclined to rain. The atmosphere felt a bit damp but it wasn't cold; it was the end of summer, after all. The last day of another mild August. Nothing would have made you think twice about getting out of bed and into the world and restarting your life from where you left it on pause last night. Nothing would have hinted it was the last day of someone else's.

When I see a bad news story now I think: what was I doing while that guy was getting kicked to death on his doorstep, or that girl was getting strangled, or that boy was fighting for his last breath in a swollen river? I was watching *The X Factor* or I was on the internet or I was

eating a biscuit and swiping the crumbs off my homework. And I never felt anything, and nor did anyone else,
and no dreadful rip opened in the fabric of space and time.
The world just went on.

In a way that's reassuring, but in another way it's terrifying. If the earth blew up tomorrow, the universe would
go on too. I can just see some little green man getting
bored with the 'Earth Explodes' breaking news, I can see
him picking up his remote and changing channels.

Maybe that's why I don't like looking at the night sky.

'Nick?'

I glanced up. On that ordinary morning I was sitting in
my usual spot against the wire fence, which was devel-
oping a baggy bit from being leaned on so often.

'Aiiidaaan . . .'

I had to say his name slowly, because I was surprised,
to put it mildly, and I had to haul myself out of the six-
teenth century before I could talk to him. I wished I'd
hidden the poetry book inside a violent graphic novel or
Loaded or something. Bad enough trying to get my head
around John Donne, who seemed to have got his head
round many things, not all of them the kind you'd discuss
with your grandmother. I'd been starting to like the man
on a personal level and I wasn't glad of an interruption
from a boy who'd never spoken a word to me in his life,
let alone a friendly one. I shut the book with a snap.
'What?'

Considering I was the one on my backside on the ground, squinting into the watery sun, Aidan was the one who looked awkward. Swinging his backpack off his shoulder, he shifted from foot to foot, then turned clumsily and crouched on his hunkers beside me. I could see him better now he wasn't standing against the diffuse sunlight and his face was on my level. He was giving me a shy sort of smile but I looked back without a word. The empty-eyed stare.

It didn't seem to faze him. 'When's Allie's birthday?'

'Why don't you ask her?'

'Because.' He looked up at the milling groups in the grounds. 'Because I don't want her to know I asked.'

'November fourth,' I said before I could stop myself.

'Thanks!' He gave me his big open grin. 'John Donne?'

I gritted my teeth. 'I have to do him. Set book. Right?'

'Right.'

'I don't read poetry.'

'Right.' He glanced idly around again. 'Orla does.'

'Is that so?' I'd have liked to hit him but that would look as if I cared what Orla did with her free time. When I followed his gaze, I saw Orla. She was standing with a bunch of girls not ten metres away. I couldn't make out whether she was looking at Aidan or at me, but whichever it was, she was finding a lot to interest her. Cold horror formed in my stomach like a lump of dirty ice, and I grabbed Aidan's sleeve and yanked him down so I could glare at him. 'I'm not reading this to impress your bloody sister.'

'Never said you were.' There was annoyance in his voice. 'Look, I know you don't like me.'

'Good.'

'And I don't like you.'

I don't know why that bald statement should hurt the way it did. I took a breath. 'And?'

'Just, Allie and me get on fine. And I hope you're not upset about it. Is all.'

I closed my book and tapped it against my knuckles. 'I'm not upset about anything.'

'Allie thinks you are.'

'She's wrong.'

'Well, will you tell her?' His expression went soft all of a sudden. I'd have liked to punch him. ''Cause she gets upset if she thinks you are.'

'Allie doesn't care what I think.'

'Yes, she does. She kind of worships you.' There was a sardonic twist to his lip.

'Not any more,' I said.

'Yes, she does. She didn't like you for a while but she changed her mind because of Shuggie and what you did.'

I sat there letting the wire fence brand a lattice pattern into my back. I was going to look like a waffle when I got up, but I needed the support and I needed the distraction. *She kind of worshipped me, but she didn't like me for a while?* I felt light-headed with relief, but there was also a terrible ache below my breastbone. *She didn't like me for a while.* Nobody had come out and said that to me before. I suppose I knew she didn't like me. I suppose nobody did. I don't suppose even Kev or Sunil or that crowd actually liked me. Fair enough: I'd never actually liked them. My last four years had been entirely empty of liking, and now Aidan didn't like me either.

Oh, so what? My phone never got nicked.

'You know my sister?' he said casually.

Knew her, feared her, fancied her. Obsessive-compulsive lust turning lately to borderline terror. But Aidan didn't have to know that, and neither did Orla. 'Yeah,' I said.

'She heard Kev saying something about you, end of last term. After you got your kicking, remember? He was kind of laughing with some guys and they were having a go at you, really loud. So she stops and taps him on the shoulder and says "At least Nick Geddes has got some balls and he doesn't keep his brains in them."'

I rolled my knuckles against John Donne's cover. 'Did she . . . um, say that, did she?'

'Uh-huh.' He'd gone a bit pink. 'Oh yeah, and then she kind of stared at his pals, and she told him his dick must be really small if he had to surround himself with bigger ones.'

I laughed out loud, couldn't help it. Then I thought about it, and laughed again. When I looked at Aidan he was smiling at me.

I scowled. 'See Allie . . .' I said.

'Uh-huh.' He tensed, and his smile vanished.

'No dumping her,' I said through my teeth. Then, because that sounded a little unreasonable, I added, 'No dumping without a good explanation and being really nice to her.'

'I'm not going to dump her,' he said.

'And you'd better look after her,' I said.

'Yes.'

'Because she goes running to you now. She doesn't come to me any more, she always goes to you, so she's your bloody responsibility. Right?'

'Yeah,' he said. And smiled. 'I'll look out for her, Nick. I promise.'

'You dropped your big white cowboy hat,' I said, and pointed across the grounds.

Taking the hint, he scrambled to his feet, grinned at me and sauntered off. I kept my glower in place till he was safely gone, so he didn't see me smile. The only person who saw that was Shuggie, hovering and watching with that bright inquiring gaze. I crooked my finger at him.

He came over and hovered some more, till I slapped the tarmac and he sat down at my side.

'Shuggie,' I said, not looking at him. 'Sometimes I think you're a bit fiendish.'

'Fiendish? What a big word, Nicholas, and difficult to spell.' He followed the direction of my stare, and before I could rip his head off said, 'There's Orla.'

Yes, there was Orla. How could my gaze go anywhere else? Aidan passed quite close to her posse and he must have said something cheeky, because she stepped smartly back, grabbed him by the lapel and mock-headbutted him. Grinning, he took her platinum forelock and tugged on it, so she slapped him on the stomach, then grabbed his head and kissed his nose.

That's your brother, I thought longingly. Don't waste all that aggressive affection on him. I can take it just as well as he can . . .

In a parallel world, one where Kev Naughton had been drowned at birth and I'd not sold my soul at the first opportune moment, I realised Aidan Mahon and I might have been friends. But as it was, that was the first time Aidan spoke to me. The day my life started to come back together, and the day it fell apart again. The last day of his life.

The last day of Aidan's life, Allie was on her own. I know what happened to her, though. Not that she told me all the details; I got those at the trial. I got the details while the jury discovered what an intimidating bruiser Aidan was, and what malicious revenge-seekers Allie and I were, and what a hard childhood Kev had had, and how much he loved his mother. Oh, don't get me started. I'll tell you what I found out, not what the jury thought.

Aidan was held up after school – not a detention, obviously, not Aidan Mahon; he'd stayed behind to discuss something with a teacher. Kev was sitting in his car, on the other side of the road, opposite the school gates, and when he saw Allie come out on her own he must have practically hit the car roof with joy. So he got out of the car and slammed the door – she heard that – and he followed her.

He was between her and the school, so she couldn't go back. So first thing she did, she pulled out her mobile and punched the speed dial. Not my number, Aidan's number. Of course. She'd only got as far as the dank copse behind the computer store before Kev caught up with her.

Kev grabbed her by the arm and yanked her into the shadow of the Amenity Value trees. Shoved her against the third tree trunk on the left – it's the details that get jammed in your brain and won't come loose – and twisted her phone out of her hand. And she thought that was it, and she didn't care about the tree bark scraping her back or the fact that her wrist hurt so much he must have sprained it. She just wanted him to go away, because she had a terrible, terrible longing for Aidan not to arrive in time: she knew in that funny old way of hers she'd made the most dreadful mistake in calling him. She just stared levelly into Kev's eyes and willed him to go away, but she didn't say anything and she didn't cry; she just felt her heart banging her ribcage and wished more than anything she hadn't called Aidan.

Kev probably sensed her terror, though he'd never have understood what lay behind it. And he wouldn't have liked her staring at him in that fearful intransigent way.

He looked left and right, gripping her phone in one hand. Then he shoved himself right against her and grabbed her breast hard with his other hand.

'Hey, Allie,' he said, so close she could feel his breath on her cheek. He smelt of cheese-and-onion crisps, she said. 'Give us a bit of what Mahon gets.' And he hit her on the cheek with her own phone, and started groping her.

He was grunting anyway, and she was frozen with horror, so she didn't realise at first when he gave a grunt of real astonishment. Somebody jerked him away from her, and he hit the ground hard.

That stunned him, but he wasn't hurt. Aidan did not hurt him. He probably thought about it, but he didn't, whatever Kev's QC said. Thinking about it isn't the same thing. Wanting to do it isn't the same thing. Wanting to kill someone isn't the same as doing it: ask my dad, who often says he'd like to kill me.

It's what you do that matters. All Aidan did was lunge for Allie's phone as Kev lay there in shock, and when he'd grabbed it he staggered back. He stared down at Kev for a few seconds, maybe not knowing what to do next, but by then Allie had had time to get her breath back and her head together, to seize his hand and tug him away. Aidan, after all, was a fifteen-year-old who'd just humiliated a sixteen-year-old, and even if he was easily as tall as Kev, he wasn't in the same psychopathic league. So after a moment he clasped Allie's hand harder, and backed away from Kev, then let Allie pull him along the path back towards the road.

Allie remembers the looming figure at the end of the path. She knows Aidan saw him too because his fingers tightened round hers and she felt him take a breath and walk faster.

Mickey Naughton had left Kev only to go and buy fags, and now he'd come to look for his brother. What he found was Kev staggering to his feet, scarlet with fury and shame, and Aidan walking away with a dishevelled girl in one hand and an unthieved phone in the other. Maybe Mickey couldn't believe what he was seeing, because Aidan had enough impetus to shove past without being grabbed, but it didn't take Mickey long to reassemble his thoughts. Kev stumbled out of the lane and Allie heard Mickey give him his unedited opinion.

'You stupit useless wee tosser! Gonnae let him get away with that?'

That's the edited version.

Allie glanced back over her shoulder to see Kev walking swiftly after them, head down, eyes up, teeth showing where they bit into his upper lip.

'Mahon,' he shouted, 'Mahon!'

Maybe Aidan thought he had to turn round or he'd be attacked from behind. So he came to a dead halt and spun on his heel.

He shouldn't have done that, but what else was he

going to do? I saw this part because by now I was running towards them, Shuggie panting at my heels. Somebody on the opposite side of the road had turned too, a tall middle-aged guy with a Jack Russell. A group of girls was walking behind me, and their laughter had faded, replaced with a bright callous curiosity, and they were striding faster towards the scrap. All I could hear in my head was the echo of my own unthinking voice: *She goes running to you now, she's your bloody responsibility.* And young Sir frigging Galahad going, *I'll look out for her, Nick. I promise.*

No, you stupid git, no, I thought. You don't know what you're getting into. Leave this to me.

As I barged past Mickey, Aidan caught sight of me. He looked back at Kev and said, 'Leave her alone.'

My words. My words exactly, give or take a gender pronoun. But this time Kev didn't take any notice; he just kept walking, head down, his whole body tight with fury, and Aidan stepped forward in front of him and the two boys collided.

I stopped. Everything stopped. I wanted to say or do something but I'd seen something for a fraction of an instant that my mind didn't want to register, a bright glint between the two of them, just before they slammed into each other. Aidan still had Allie's phone in one hand but his other arm was up to grab Kev, ready to stop him in his tracks. And he did stop him. Kev just stood, frozen to Aidan, while Aidan stared into his face, looking very surprised. Then Aidan's eyes slewed across to me, full of a sort of hurt bewilderment.

He started to slide. He glanced down, then back up at Kev, trying to hold himself up, but Kev wasn't helping, he just stood there like a piece of meat. Aidan slid to his knees and let go of Kev.

I only knew about the silence when Mickey broke it.

'That wis self-defence.' He strode up and grabbed Kev's arms, manhandling him away. 'That wis fecking self-defence.'

I didn't care what it was. I was still trying to work out what had happened, while in another layer of my mind I knew fine. Also I was trying to keep hold of my phone, which had appeared in my palm somehow, but it kept slipping in my damp shaking hand while I tried to thumb buttons.

Allie was on the pavement now with Aidan in her arms. He'd slumped back into her lap and he was looking up at her, the bewilderment turned into terror, his knees drawn up, his hands clutched over a spot below his breastbone, blood pumping out between his fingers. He kept slumping sideways like he just couldn't stop himself, and Allie held on to him and stroked his hair and went, 'Sh, sh.'

There was the slam of a car door, the phlegmy roar of a souped-up engine and the screech of departing tyres. Someone was nagging and badgering me through the phone that was stuck to my ear, but I couldn't make out

what they were saying, because someone else was shouting obscenities as she shoved through the gathering
crowd. Orla bumped into me, knocking the phone out of
my hand, but it was fine because there were plenty of
people making calls. She fell silent, then she screamed.

Allie didn't scream and she didn't shout. She sat as
Aidan's body jerked in her arms and his blood pooled
around her legs, as his life soaked out of him and through
her trousers and into her skin. Her eyes were the colour
of night, and she was still hushing him softly. She cradled
him like a baby, and until the sirens drowned her out, I
heard her whispering that he wasn't going to die, because
she wasn't going to let him.

And I suppose she never did.

NOW

14

Aloof, swotty, aggressive. What a combination. She didn't give a damn, did Orla. Those terrifying, black-rimmed eyes. Her strong defiant body with its eff-you language, her proud breasts, her barbaric nose ring. Orla, Orla. That flick of platinum hair falling across one eye like a cool blade. I could smell her gum across the chipped formica table in the Soda Fountain. I could smell the mint of it on her breath, mixed with cigarettes and espresso. I could eat her in one bite. Or die trying. More likely.

'How come you get to climb over that fence lunchtimes?' I asked her.

'McCluskey.'

'McCluskey what?'

Shrugging, Orla stared over my shoulder at the window, as if she was less interested in me than in the backwards writing that said *Beppe's Soda Fountain* from the front.

'Says I can go over there at the moment. Just at the moment, mind. If I want some privacy. 'Cause of . . .'

'Yeah,' I said. 'Just you, though? Not Gina or Kylie or that lot?'

She sniffed. 'That crowd of losers? I'm sick of them.'

If they could hear her! 'Do they know that?'

'Nah. Back to normal next week, right?' She gazed at me, daring me ever to tell them what she'd said about her own hard glamorous gang.

As if I'd take my life in my hands like that.

'McCluskey's OK for a fascist bastard,' I said.

'Yeah.' She tugged out a cigarette.

If I was switched on – if I was a smoker – I'd have had a light ready for her. The Soda Fountain was the kind of place to play James Dean or John Travolta, a faux-fifties diner done up in pastel ice-cream colours and chrome. It was full of kitsch, like the straw dispenser and the bubblegum machine and the jukebox full of music we didn't like. There was a papier-mâché Chevrolet on the counter, Neapolitan pink, and black-and-white film stills on the walls. If I was playing my role, I'd lean forward and gaze into Orla's black-edged eyes as she bent her head low and touched her fag to my flame, then glanced up at me from beneath her thick lashes.

But I'm not switched on, I'm not cool, and unfortunately I'm not a smoker.

'Can I have one of those?'

'No.' She twirled her unlit cigarette between her

fingers, her stare full of pity and scorn. 'Neither can I.'

Oh aye. Smoking ban. I felt like an idiot. Again.

'Filthy stupid habit, anyway,' she said. 'Looks stupid, is stupid. Can I have another coffee?'

Beneath the cover of the table I opened my fist and peered at what was left of my cash. Hell, it was an investment. 'Yeah. OK. How do you sleep nights?'

'How do you?'

The silence was as thick as Beppe's espresso, and just about as dark. I stood up and went to the counter and mumbled a new order. Beppe gave me a baleful look – he always looked Mafia-malevolent so nobody would take the mickey out of his wee fifties-diner busboy hat and stripey apron – and obliged.

It took all my nerve to sit back down opposite Orla, but I managed it, and even looked up at her. Her mouth was sullen but her eyes glittered with interest. OK.

'You used to hang out with him.'

Him. Kev Naughton. Well, that was getting to the point.

'Yeah, well,' I said. 'Not any more.'

'Yeah, but you used to. I don't think much of your taste in friends.'

Like I needed to hear that again. Anger made me snap, 'He used to fancy you.'

She didn't stop staring at me. 'Yeah.' Her lips parted and her teeth sank into her lower lip. She bit it harder. I could see the mark she was making. 'I told him I wasn't interested.'

'You grabbed his nuts and twisted, Orla.'

I'd thought it was funny then and I thought it was funny now. Because I was trying not to smile too much I glanced over her shoulder at the sugar-pink Chevy. She didn't say anything though, and when I looked back at her I realised I'd never imagined Orla Mahon could cry.

Her eyes were very glittery and she put a black finger-nail to the corner of each one, staring at the table. I realised the polish wasn't quite black: it was very, very dark red. I wished I hadn't made her cry. I couldn't look away from her fingernails.

'I don't,' I said. 'I don't . . . you don't need to . . .' My throat dried up.

'I don't feel guilty,' she snapped, taking her fingers down so she could glare at me. Now she was angry enough not to cry.

'I didn't say you –'

'Even if Kev was getting his own back. Even if he started on Aidan 'cause . . . 'cause I did that to him. In front of everybody. I shouldn't've. Well, whether I should or not . . . it's no excuse for . . . It's no *excuse*. I didn't *make* him do it. Did I? *Did I?*'

'No,' I said. 'Course not. Kev did it. All by himself.'

'I don't feel guilty about anything. I don't even feel that guilty about being alive. I just feel really, really bad that he's dead. And that makes me feel a bit guilty. See? That's it. Don't know why. See?'

No, Orla, not really. 'Yeah.'

'It's still August,' she said.

Whatever that had to do with anything. 'Uh-huh . . .'

She smiled at me, very suddenly and disarmingly.

'Fancy a swim?'

15

If Orla had not been there, I'd never have taken off my clothes.

Those are thirteen lovely words. Unfortunately it was a lot less exciting than it sounds, and a great deal more uncomfortable, because all it involved was getting mad-bugger cold and wet. First of all we sat on the sea wall for a while, leaning our arms on the rusty handrail till our backsides were numb and pockmarked from the lumpy bits in the concrete. I was hoping she'd start to shiver, so I could yawn and stretch and put my arm round her shoulder, but it wasn't cold enough to carry that off, and I vividly recalled what had happened to Kev. She was kind of preoccupied, anyway, texting her mother for the umpteenth time to say she was all right. After a bit she snapped her phone shut and put another bit of gum in her mouth. The old bit, wrapped up in a bus ticket, she flicked down on to the hard-packed sand beyond the shingle.

The tide was quite far out, the sea calm and glossy black. Sluggish waves thumped on to the shore fifty metres away, lacy foam just licking the end of the breakwater. Out towards the harbour, light glowed white and orange, but in front of us all was blackness. There were no stars reflected in the sea. If there were any in the sky, you couldn't see them for the glare of the town.

In the winter, I remembered, when the north-east wind was whipping ice crystals across the esplanade, you could put your bare hand on this railing and it would stick. You'd have to pull it off and leave skin behind. What made me think of that?

I risked a sideways glance. 'See that nose ring?'

'Uh-huh.' Orla didn't turn.

'Well. When it's cold. I mean really cold. Does it, like, give you ice burns?'

Her body sagged against the railing, world-weary. Resting her head on her arms, she flopped it sideways to give me a look of withering disbelief.

I guess that was a no, then.

'Nice night,' she said.

'Water'll be freezing,' I said.

'Tough guy,' she said. 'I thought you were going to swim?'

I thought you were going to as well. I just said, 'Yeah,' and pulled my T-shirt over my head, then pulled myself up by the railings and toed off my trainers. Then I yanked off my socks one at a time. I was switched on enough to know that it's socks before jeans, to avoid looking a complete prat. After the jeans, though, that would be the tricky part. That would be the moment of decision, so I left them on for the time being.

I ducked under the railings and lowered myself down with one hand. The sea wall was about four metres high and kind of steep, with stones set into the concrete. I could push myself away, try to run down and probably smack face-first into the shingle. Or I could let go and drop. It would have been smarter and cooler to go round to the steps, of course, but too late to think about being smart. Instead I chose the lesser of two evils, letting go of the rail and half sliding, half falling to the beach. It was relatively graceful, I suppose, and I managed not to howl when the sea wall took a layer of skin off my ribs.

I looked up. Orla was looking down. I could see her mouth moving round the gum.

'You coming?'

'In a minute,' she said. Taking her gum out of her mouth, she stuck it on the railing. A light flared, casting a glow across her face, and the tip of a cigarette burned fierce and bright.

Peeling off my jeans, I stood for an uncertain moment. It would be cooler and harder to take off my underpants too. It would also be that tiny degree more painful when I went in the sea.

I decided I did not look nonchalant enough, standing there in my underwear; in fact there was a touch of prissiness about it. What the hell. With a last quick check for passers-by – I didn't want to be arrested – I took off my underpants too. Best to get this over with quickly, then. Without a backward glance at Orla, I bolted down the sand and into the water, plunging through till the depth and the temperature finally slowed me down.

Mustn't squeal, I thought, gritting my teeth. How girly would that be?

It wasn't so bad. Not once I was in. It was August, and anyway there comes a point when you're too numb to feel it any more. I did a few frantic strokes to warm myself up, then trod water, rubbed seawater out of my face and stared back at the distant glow of Orla's fag. Now that I wasn't feeling the cold so much, I could feel the salt stinging the lovely new scrape down my side. That was going to look great in the morning.

I floated on to my back and stared up. Honestly, I was beginning to enjoy myself now. The waves were soothingly small, rocking me, splashing my face, so I closed my eyes, and when I opened them again I saw there were stars after all. You could see them from out here, or maybe my eyes had adjusted. I could make out Orion's left foot, maybe, and something that might or might not have been a Plough or a Bear – I'm not good with stars – and there was a broad arc of lighter darkness. It might have been the Milky Way; it might have been the reflected glow of a million street lights. I stared up into the darkness, contemplating the universe, needing Orla suddenly like I needed to breathe. How else could anyone stand being so small and transient? Only by being alive and shouting your head off at the gods and reproducing your genes when you got a chance.

Um. But maybe hold the reproduction for a bit . . .

Splashing upright, I faced a shore that seemed a lot further away. I could have been floating in space at that moment, trying to breathe in a vacuum, and I was terribly lonely.

Scared, too. I could no longer see the bright burning tip of a cigarette; I could no longer see a hunched silhouette against the street-lit glare of the esplanade. Was she too far away, or was she gone? My limbs felt heavy and numb, as if they might grow waterlogged and drag me under, and I could no longer feel the sting of my scraped side.

I took a few strokes into the lapping waves, thinking I might drift back towards shore, but I didn't. The sea was calm but wasn't there an undertow in this bay? What was going on beneath the surface? I started to shiver again as the cold reached my bones, and then I started to panic. And I still couldn't see Orla. What had happened to Orla?

Treading water furiously, I tried to warm myself up so I could swim. Of course there was a sodding undertow. I couldn't feel it; it simply drew me out and further out. Some student drowned last summer, I remembered. Some guy who was too stupid to know any better . . . I tried not to think about it. Instead I peered up and down the beach, screwing up my eyes into the white glare above the sea wall and the contrasting dark shadows beneath.

Now I could see a different shape of darkness moving. She had come down the concrete steps, like anyone sensible would, and was crouching down to something on the beach. Her shape was all wrong and it took me a bit of time to make out that the stick figure held an armful of clothing. My clothes. She'd come down to the beach to get my jeans and my underpants. I thought I could see my trainers, hooked into two fingers of one hand.

She stopped and looked out towards me. At least, I think she did. She seemed to do that, but no way could I see the expression on her face.

My legs were flailing in the water now. I was cold, and scared, and ragingly angry, not so much with her as with myself. It's the oldest one in the book, Nick. The oldest one in the book. How are you going to get home now? Make that, how are you planning to get home assuming you avoid both drowning and hypothermia? Furious, I was furious. How could you imagine she wanted you for your scintillating company? Oh, why not just drown, Nicholas, and avoid the humiliation?

The darkness that was Orla moved, turned, headed for the steps. She didn't even dignify me by giving me the finger; for Orla Mahon, as she climbed the steps and left me to sink in my own stupidity, I no longer even existed. Her shadow moved, onwards and upwards, up towards the esplanade, leaving me in the lightless starless sea.

At the railing she hesitated and turned to me again. I think she did. It was hard to tell.

Laying down the armful of clothes, she stood up, a normal shape again in the white glow of street lighting. She walked back down the steps and then all the way to the water's edge, till I thought I could make out her features once more. Still couldn't read them, but at least I could see black-rimmed eyes in a pale hard beautiful face. I thought I caught the tiny glint of a nose ring in the light of what might have been the Milky Way. But she was far away, so far away. I probably imagined how she looked. My imaginary girlfriend.

'You OK?' she called.

'Yes.' I couldn't say more for my chattering teeth, and I didn't want to betray myself. I decided I had better die with dignity. Water slapped innocuously at my shoulders as the gentle sea pulled me ever further out into silence and space. It was so quiet I could hear waves hitting the shore, so far away.

She stared out to sea, while the distant thud and rush of the waves echoed in my head and made it throb. I wished it would stop so I could hear her breathing. At this distance? Stupid thing to wish for. Like I mattered a damn to a relentless sea, on an indifferent planet, in the middle of an unimaginable universe. Suddenly I felt like crying.

'You're too far out,' she called.

'No I'm not.'

Thud. Rush. Whisper of surf over shingle.

'You are.'

Thud. Rush. Whisper. Thud. Rush. Whisper.

'Swim back in a bit.'

No, I was about to yell, but my head was pounding with coffee and cold fear. Trying to look leisurely, I took a few strokes towards shore. Then a few more, faster and stronger, fighting the tide properly. I gasped, got a mouthful of North Sea, and panicked. As luck would have it, my body's response to panic was to strike out in a flailing ungainly crawl towards Orla, instead of just thrashing around till I sank. Ten more metres, and another ten. After longer than I liked, I felt my toes sink and scrabble in sand. Two more strokes. Panic, that was all. The suck of the tide had been gentler than I deserved, and I was back in my depth.

Orla took a step back. I watched her. I was still a good way from shore. How fast could I run, chest-deep in the water? Could I reach her running before she got to the steps? Could I bring her down in the sand before she escaped on to the esplanade?

No, I decided. I dug my toes deeper in the drifting sand, but stayed in the water up to my neck, moving my arms beneath the inky surface, pretending I was still treading water even as I edged closer to her. She took another step back. She was on to me.

'Orla,' I said.

'What?'

I wanted to say *Please don't do this,* or *Eff off before I kill you,* but I couldn't decide on which, so I didn't say either. She just stood there motionless.

After a bit she tilted her head, gripped her hair in one fist and brought it down in front of her shoulder, then started to twist it into a long braid. And I just watched her do it, because it was fascinating.

The mad thing was, I was still fantasising about rugby-tackling her and bringing her down into the sand, but not because I was angry.

When she came to the end of her braid she let it hang unsecured as she shrugged off her jacket and let it flop to the sand. Under it she was wearing a strappy top with a diamante star right between her breasts. Her bra straps showed and so did her navel, where another little metal ring glinted. Orla was not skinny or toothpicky but her flesh didn't bulge out over her belt: her stomach just looked as hard and strong and solid as the rest of her. I swallowed, got another mouthful of sea, and choked. My limbs had gone all numb again.

She kicked off her sandals and tugged off her skirt, but to my chagrin she didn't take off the cropped top or her underwear. She waded into the water, hesitated, then waded further. She didn't look at me. She didn't shiver, or gasp, or squeal. She just kept wading till the water was up to her thighs and her waist and her ribcage, and then she pushed herself forward and swam into my arms.

I almost forgot to put them round her, I was so shocked.

But I did. I felt her arms go round my back, too, and I shivered again.

'You're cold,' she said, just as I said, 'It's not that cold.'

Her pigtail floated out beside her head, not unravelling, staying together, a fat sleek watersnake rising and falling with the black waves. I eyed it, hypnotised, then turned my gaze back to her face. Orla Mahon's face, and it was a hand's breadth away from mine. I looked at her nose ring, and then at her black-edged eyes, and then at her mouth. Which opened slightly. I saw her tongue run across her teeth. And then she kissed me.

I'll have to repeat that. Orla Mahon *kissed me.*

Oh, God. She tasted of spearmint and Silk Cut and watermelon lipgloss. She tasted like everything I ever wanted in my whole life. There was a helpless little whimper of lust, and that came from me. At least the sea was cold enough to stop me making a complete idiot of myself. If you see what I mean.

The sea. Cold! My stomach plummeted. I hoped to God I hadn't shrunk.

As I tensed, anxious, Orla drew away, studying my face bit by bit. She took my skull in both hands. I stumbled in clumsy slow motion, regaining my footing in the yielding sand just in time for her to put her lips to my cheekbone, right under my eye socket. Her lips lingered, then she licked them.

'Salty,' she said. 'That the sea?'

'Yes,' I lied. It was too much to explain, all that about

being small and transient and mortal in a very big universe.

'Yes,' said Orla, and kissed my other cheekbone.

I tightened my arms around her body. I didn't dare touch her breasts but my palms stroked her ribs and her shoulder blades and her upper arms, and the strong solid flesh that covered them.

'I thought you were going to steal my clothes,' I mumbled.

'I was,' said Orla.

'Uh-huh,' I said.

'That's before I thought you were going to drown, you stupid git.'

'Uh-huh.'

'It isn't that cold at all,' said Orla. 'Is it?'

'No,' I said. I kissed her again. My tongue found hers. Just to see if that was pierced, too. It wasn't. No stud or anything. I checked it again. Just in case I'd missed something.

Orla's fingers stroked down my chest, making me shudder with something that wasn't cold. Her strong hands moved out across my ribcage to hold my torso. I thought I was going to die of happiness, and I didn't want to wince, but I couldn't help it, because her black-glossed nails had scraped across my side.

'What's wrong?'

'Nothing,' I lied, then added: ''Tis but a scratch.'

She thought that was funny, and smiled, so I decided

she must like me a bit, because I'd never heard anything so lame in my life.

'We'd better get out,' she said.

'I'm not bothered,' I said. I touched her hard belly with my fingertips, fascinated by the little ring.

'You're about to get hypothermia,' said Orla. 'And it might be polluted and you'll get blood poisoning and die.'

I thought about that. 'OK,' I said.

'And I have to go home.' She backed away but caught my hand and kept holding it as she pulled me after her out of the water. She kept holding it as she picked up her jacket and rubbed herself dry after a fashion, then had a half-hearted go at me too. Which I liked. She only let go of my hand to tug her skirt back on, then she took her sandals in one hand and got my hand back with the other. We walked back up the beach like that and I thought, if anybody sees us I'm going to be arrested.

She let go of my hand again at the steps, watched my eyes for a couple of seconds, then climbed the steps alone. I stood there and let her. She could have got away, now that I wasn't going to drown after all, but she didn't try. She picked up the bundle of clothes by the railing and brought them down to me.

Brassily Orla watched me get dressed, then marched back up the concrete steps. I think she was wondering if she'd been too soft on me. Handed a chance to humiliate me or drown me, she'd decided to kiss me instead, and maybe she felt she'd betrayed someone, because at the top of the steps she stared in the direction of town and said, 'Don't talk about my brother.'

'Fine,' I said.

'Or about your sister.'

'OK.'

'In fact, just don't talk.'

Which I could have taken for a brush-off, except that she took my hand again and wound her fingers into mine, and she didn't let go of it all the way home.

16

It was well after midnight when I closed the door behind me, so I was surprised the light was still on in the kitchen. Mum liked an early bed and Dad, though he stayed up late, usually slumped with his nightcap in the front room, watching late-night Film Four. I didn't want to know what was going on so I headed quietly for the stairs, but I must have made some kind of noise, because the kitchen door opened very suddenly.

Dad stood there staring at me. It was a Shugs-without-the-glasses stare, his eyes focusing on a point ten centimetres beyond my actual face. His ponytail was coming loose from its elastic band and I realised the ashy fairness had, in the last few months, been threaded with true grey. His lips were tight and trembling and he looked very thin, so that his artfully ripped jeans hung unflatteringly low on his hips and his faded Che Guevara T-shirt looked baggy. His ill-aimed gaze was accusing.

'You kids,' he said. 'You bloody kids.'

I could still feel the imprint of Orla's lips on my lips, and on my cheekbones, and on my neck. I wanted to go up to my room and lie like a corpse on my bed, not moving, so I could enjoy the lingering tactile memory. I wanted to imagine that wild, extravagant sex she insisted I was never going to get.

But Dad was still glaring at me. Mum had come to his shoulder, but he was obstructing her and now he gripped her hand, demanding parental solidarity. Oh, yeah. I was fluent in the two-way sign language they thought so cryptic and private.

Mum curled her fingers round his. 'Where have you been, Nick? What have you been doing?'

'How's that your business?'

'How dare you tell your mother –'

'Nick, love, I'm not trying to give you a hard time, I just –'

'Is it Allie?' I interrupted. I didn't care what they thought of me. I didn't care what they thought I'd been up to; I just knew suddenly that this was something to do with Allie and we were wasting time here. I thought about shops and security guards. I thought about train tracks and cuttings. And then, oh God, I remembered Mickey. My thoughts were quick and savage and scary. 'Is it Allie, Mum?'

'What would you care?' snapped Dad.

'What?'

The injustice of it took my breath away. I felt the blood drain out of my face, and my head whirled.

'Terence, that's not fair. You mustn't –'

'What's she done?' I said.

'Who?'

'Allie. What's she done?'

'Allie?' Dad cried angrily. 'Allie? Allie hasn't done anything. It's you. You. You bloody neds. You *yobs*. Work it out or go and ask your pals, *Nicholas*. Go and ask them.'

Yeah: what pals would those be, *Father*? How would he not know I was gangless and friendless? I'd kind of assumed he knew, and I was shocked to realise he didn't. So was Mum, by the look on her face. Swallowing, she looked from him to me and back again.

'You bastard,' I shouted, incoherent, inarticulate, unimaginative. 'You *bastard*.'

Had he forgotten? Or did the whole destruction of my life not make a blip on his Allie-centred radar? I wondered how to ask him which it was. I wondered how he knew even less about me than I thought he did. Imagine that being possible.

But his eyes were brimming with maudlin anger, and I didn't get a chance to say another word, and nor did Mum. He slammed the door in my face.

I whacked my fists against it. Then again, and again. I punched that door till it hurt – a lot – but I didn't try to open it. If I opened it I'd kill him.

Through the door I heard Mum's anguished sound of protest, then a half-hearted argument, but Dad was in high dudgeon and she was choosing not to damage his precarious pride or rub salt in his wounded feelings. I knew she wouldn't come out and talk to me because, after all, I was tough and Dad was fragile. I could take it, Dad was older and he couldn't. I had the resilience of youth and a rhino skin; he needed his dignity, some respect, he needed the prop of her loyalty and adoration because when did he ever get that from bloody Nick?

Besides, Mum's Words of sodding Wisdom didn't cover every eventuality and even if they did, she'd be wasting them on me. Wouldn't she? I shoved away from the door and stood in a daze in the hall, waiting for the world to make sense again. Well, that would be a long wait.

My gullet felt knotted and I couldn't see or breathe well. After a bit, though, I found I was still breathing and that I could focus clearly enough to hate the flower-sprigged wallpaper, and the calendar with the dolphin photos, and by the time I was hating those viciously enough, I found I could hate Dad. The hate was unencumbered. There wasn't room to like him any more, let alone love him. I couldn't feel Orla's kiss now, not anywhere. I felt like I'd been slapped and I wanted to go into the kitchen and hit him back, so I made myself climb the stairs one at a painful time till I got to the middle landing, and then I did it again till I got to the top. There. That wasn't so hard.

I stopped at Allie's door. Princess. Little Geddes goddess. My scraped side stung like hell, and so did my eyes. Instead of knocking gently, checking inside to make sure she was asleep – she always was, calm and conscienceless as a cat on standby – I shut my own door with something like a slam, got into my T-shirt and pyjama bottoms and crawled under my duvet.

From beneath ten-and-a-half togs I heard my door open quietly and close again, so I crammed my duvet against my ears and lay still. My teeth were gritted and I was holding my breath. Hey, Dad, guess what! Tonight I nearly drowned in the sea. Tonight I was kissed by the girl of my dreams. If you knew, would you have worried? If I'd told you, would you be happy for me? Annoyingly, tears were leaking out of my stinging eyes and soaking into the mattress, but I wasn't sobbing or bubbling or anything stupid. I didn't wonder who was in the room because I didn't care.

Somebody sat down beside me; I knew it because the mattress sagged. 'Nick?'

Little goddess, little bitch. I ignored her; maybe she'd go away.

Fat chance. '*Nick.*' She tugged at a fistful of duvet. Then at two fistfuls.

'Nick, stop crying and *talk to me.*'

Rubbing my eyes hurriedly on my T-shirt, I flung off the duvet and glared at her. 'I'm not crying. Eff off, Allie. I've had it for tonight. Just piss off and leave me alone.'

'I reckon you get enough of that,' she said.

I glared at her some more. 'That wanker downstairs,' I said. 'That tosser. That bastard.'

'I know,' she said.

'Where's Aidan?' I snapped. 'Go and talk to fecking Aidan.'

'He's not here.' Allie reached out tentatively and stroked the hair at my temple like I always did for her, only it didn't really work because my hair was so short. 'This is none of Aidan's business.'

I hesitated, taken aback.

'It's nothing to do with Aidan,' she said again. 'This is you and me.'

She'd got me in a soft spot. I leaned back on my elbows, fists clenched tight, and ground my teeth less angrily. 'Did something happen today?'

'Between me and Aidan? Sort of.'

'No, Allie, for God's *sake.* In real life. Did something just *happen*?'

'Yeah,' she said. 'Yeah.' Glancing up at me from beneath her blunt spikes of hair, she nibbled on her thumbnail, her manga eyes big and nervous. 'Never mind that, Nick, I want to talk about you. Did you meet Orl—'

'Allie, shut up! What happened to you?' I was tempted to grab her, but that might scare her away, so I sat forward, dug my fingers into my upper arms and tried to hold her with my gaze. It was OK, though: she wasn't trying to escape. She only looked sheepish.

'I lost my phone,' she said.

'You what?'

'I lost my –'

'Yeah, yeah. I mean, how?'

Nibble, nibble on the thumbnail. 'Well. Somebody took it.'

'*What?*'

'I don't mind, Nick. Don't get angry, please.'

'Who was it?' I was trying not to yell but I wasn't doing very well. Mickey, had Mickey hurt her?

'Just some kids. Please don't get angry. I didn't like it. I didn't want it, I never used it.'

Quite. That was true, and I knew why. Look what happened last time.

I made a big effort to keep my voice down. 'Who was it, Allie? Honest, I won't lose my temper. Please tell me who.'

She shrugged. 'Didn't know them.'

I thought about the swaggering Reservoir Puppies on the High Street that day. Could have been them. Could have been anyone. 'Didn't you?' I asked darkly.

'No. I didn't. That's true, honest.'

'Well, bloody Dad seems to think it was me.'

'Dad's a bit irrational at the moment.' Nibble nibble. 'He was upset.'

'Princess,' I said. 'Goddess.'

'Yeah. I know.' She took her thumbnail out of her mouth. 'I'm sorry, Nick. Sorry about that.'

'It's not your fault.' I had never thought so, and I wasn't about to start now. 'It's OK.'

We sat there in silence. I didn't feel so much like crying any more. The atmosphere was quite easy, considering I was blazingly angry.

'Did you get hurt?'

'Not really.' She pulled her pyjama sleeve down over her knuckles and I frowned, noticing for the first time the dressing on her hand. 'Just my hand, a bit. They dragged it out of my hand and it scraped on a wall. That's all.'

Which meant, in Allie-speak, that they'd slammed it against the wall and it was badly grazed. Before I could stop myself it was out. 'So where was your Aidan then?'

She didn't withdraw, all cold and hurt. She didn't bite my head off. She said, 'He was scared, you can't blame him. Of course he was scared.'

I nearly said: *Yeah, but that's hardly going to happen to him twice . . .*

I bit my tongue and restrained myself. Instead I said, 'I wish you could let him go.'

'So do I,' she said.

There didn't seem to be anything more to say, so we sat in our companionable silence for a while. Downstairs we could hear the parents moving around, subdued, uncommunicative. I heard the recognisable plop of a cork coming out of a bottle. A new one? At this time of night?

Not long afterwards the stairs creaked beneath Mum's tired tread, and then came the light drum roll of her fingertips against Allie's door on the other side of the landing.

Allie's eyes met mine and we held our breaths.

'Allie?' said Mum.

Allie's door creaked open. Silence. Then, very softly, it was closed again. Mum paused in the hallway outside my room and Allie clamped her lips together as if she might giggle. When I scowled she put her hand over her mouth, but her eyes were still crinkled with laughter. Grinning, I crossed the fingers of both hands.

Mum must know what she ought to do now. Mum must know that she ought to come in here and talk to us, talk about Dad being frightened and upset and that's why he'd behaved so badly towards me, it wasn't the wine, it wasn't his late nights, and he'd say sorry in the morning: yes, she'd make sure this time he did. She should come in now, matter of fact and maternal, and say Allie mustn't have nightmares, and the phone didn't matter and Mum was just glad she hadn't been hurt any worse than some skinned knuckles. She should come in and do a bit of bonding and give us one or two of her priceless Words of Wisdom.

Allie and I looked at each other, praying through our stifled giggles that she'd be too embarrassed or afraid even to try. For once the gods took pity on me, or maybe on Allie, because Mum abruptly pushed open her own bedroom door, making crystals tinkle, and shut it firmly behind her. After a moment we heard the clatter of her wardrobe door and the murmur of her bedside radio, the creak of her mattress and the click of her lamp.

'Thank Gawd for that,' breathed Allie, and grinned at me.

I was happy, I thought suddenly. Just for tonight, I was happy. Allie was sitting on my bed, giggling with me and being rude about the parents. I hadn't drowned. And Orla kissed me. Orla Mahon kissed *me*.

'Orla kissed me,' I said. Well, I had to tell someone.

'Oh! Good! I thought she was going to be horrible to you.'

'Well, she was,' I admitted. 'But she kissed me too.'

Allie laughed behind her hand. 'You and Orla Mahon. What's Aidan going to say?'

'Aidan,' I echoed. The fizz had gone out of the atmosphere, and I rubbed my hand across my head. I didn't want to hurt Allie's feelings but I didn't want Aidan to have anything to do with me and Orla. I wanted him to stay out of it.

'You know, I'm nearly the same age as him now. I'm catching up.'

I was annoyed enough to argue. 'Aidan would still be two years older than you.'

'If he'd lived.' She shrugged at my headboard.

'Yeah, if he'd lived.'

'But he didn't,' she said. 'He stopped.'

'He stopped,' I echoed. Funny way of putting it.

Catching the impatience in my voice, she shook her

head. 'Forget Aidan. Sorry.'

'Allie,' I said, nipping my lip. 'Why does he have to stay?'

'I don't know.' Allie peered at the floor. In the room below the television chuntered, the sofa creaked and there was the chink of a bottleneck against a wine glass. She looked quickly back at me. 'I owe him my life.'

I opened my mouth, then closed it again. What did that mean, really? *I owe him my life.* If you owed somebody something, didn't you have to hand it over in the end? Did she just mean she was grateful? Or was it that she shouldn't be alive since he was dead because of her? *I owe him my life.* Did that mean one day she'd have to pay up?

She didn't owe him any such thing. She'd made up this story in her head to make Aidan's death worthwhile, when it was only stupid and pointless and evil. Of course, she felt guilty for phoning him: that I could understand. That's why she told herself she owed Aidan her life. I only hoped she hadn't recreated him so that one day he could come and collect it.

'Be careful,' I told her.

Smiling, she planted a kiss on my forehead, then jumped down off the bed. On the way out she stuck her head back round my door.

'OK,' she said. 'I promise, Nick. I promise I'll be careful.'

And that, for the moment, was going to have to do.

17

Look what happened last time. Yeah, quite.

Maybe it was me who owed Aidan my life. If it had been my number on Allie's speed dial, it might have been me jerking on the ground in a puddle of my own blood.

I think that had occurred to Orla, too. This made it all the more amazing that one year on I was sitting in the musty darkness of the local cinema, my forearm warm against hers where we'd come to some unspoken agreement about personal space after a little awkward elbowing. The film might have been tedious or it might not; I wouldn't know, because I'd spent the first half-hour watching Orla's face out of the corner of my eye. I liked seeing the blue shadows move across her skin, liked seeing her muscles tighten into tiny smiles and frowns; I even liked watching them settle into rigid boredom. I liked the way her fingers slid popcorn in her mouth, liked watching her lips part a little as she chewed.

'Good show?' she murmured after a bit.

'Yeah,' I said.

The corner of her mouth twitched up into a knowing smile and she nudged the carton of popcorn in my direction.

'No thanks.' I nudged it back and it tipped and tumbled to the ground, spilling popcorn round her feet like a shower of dull gold. Chewing her last piece, she slanted her eyes at me.

'Sorry,' I said.

Her face flickered with the shadows of the screen as she watched me, her mouth curving in a broad smile. 'Nice one.'

Yeah, well, it had got the stupid popcorn out of the way. Leaning down half-heartedly, I scrabbled for the bits that weren't in contact with the grubby floor. Nobody had been allowed to smoke in here for years, so how come the floor still smelt like an unwashed ashtray?

'Forget it,' she murmured. 'I'm not eating that.'

In front of us a lady shifted in her seat and cleared her throat. It silenced me, because for a moment there I'd forgotten we were in a public place.

Dropping a few retrieved nuggets of popcorn back to the floor, I uncurled, stretched lazily and rather obviously, and laid my arm across Orla's shoulders. I tensed my jaw for a slap, and my balls shrank a bit in expectation.

She didn't hit them or me. Her body sagged against

mine, and I gave a silent sigh of relief while my heart bounced against my lungs. It made it hard to breathe but I managed, even though her hand now lay lightly against my inner thigh.

My breathing sounded kind of squeaky, so I tried not to think about where Orla's hand was, and watched the screen instead. I wondered why those people there were doing that, and what they were talking about, and why they were now running like the clappers, and why I hadn't paid attention for the first half-hour.

No, I knew that bit.

'Who's that?' I hissed at Orla, nodding at the face now filling the screen.

She gave me a disbelieving look. 'Matt Damon.'

'No, I mean who *is* he?'

'Haven't you watched this *at all*?'

I gave her my best sheepish smile, and she laughed through her nose. I liked the way that made her whole face crinkle up.

The woman in front heaved her shoulders and gave a loud exasperated sigh. I was looking at a neat woollen jacket collar, a tightly-sprayed hairdo and a row of pearls. I wondered if I could throttle her with the pearls. I made practice motions with my hands, twisting my face into a demented scowl, and got an elbow in the ribs from Orla.

'Nick!' she whispered, and frowned at me.

'Well, I mean . . .'

The elegant dame's tolerance must have been strained

beyond bearing, because she turned in her seat and eyed me like a professional hitman. She had pearls in her ears, too. She looked like the Queen or something.

'Excuse me.' Her voice rang out, clear and genteel. 'But I'd be awfully grateful if you two would shut the feck up.'

Except she didn't say 'feck'.

'Sorry!' The word came out of Orla's throat all strangled. Grabbing my hand, she hauled me out of my seat. It banged up on its spring, and our feet crunched on popcorn, and I was bashing my thighs on every seat in the row as she tugged me along. I felt terribly guilty about the noise now but at least we were leaving. Yep, we obviously were. Orla dragged me out into the foyer like some rampaging cavewoman; she'd have had me by the hair if I'd had enough of it. I was quite enjoying being manhandled.

In the foyer she shoved me against the Coke machine. 'I am never,' she snarled, '*never* going to the movies with you *ever* again.'

'Oh,' I said lamely.

'I *hate* people that talk over films.'

She must have been really mad at me because her body was pressed against mine. It was turning my bones to porridge and at the same time it was all that was propping me up. I smiled at her. I couldn't help it.

'I like you, though,' she added as an afterthought. 'Buy me a coffee.'

It wasn't a request, it was an order. I didn't take orders.

'You can kiss my . . .'

Her mouth closed on my mouth and I forgot what I was going to say. I never knew I liked popcorn so much. I took her face in my hands and held it still so that I could taste her better. Salted popcorn, the best kind. Salted popcorn and lipgloss.

The woman in the ticket kiosk cleared her throat, but I didn't want to take my tongue out of Orla's mouth where it was getting acquainted with hers. I didn't want to let go of her head, because my thumbs were stroking the contours and hollows of her ears and I hadn't finished yet; there was a little fold in the skin at the top of each ear and it was fascinating. Ticket Woman cleared her throat more violently and threw us a glare. I drew away from Orla and sighed. The sigh came out in a rush because it was the first time I'd breathed for a while.

'You given up the fags?' I asked.

'Trying.'

'Nice,' I said, licking my lips.

Orla cast a dagger glare at Ticket Woman. 'Throat-clearing is passive-aggressive behaviour. I liked the Pearly Queen a lot better.'

I nodded, smiling stupidly at her. I don't think I've ever done as much smiling-like-an-idiot in my life, and my face was aching with the unaccustomed exercise.

'We're behaving antisocially,' she added loudly. 'We'd better go deal some drugs and break some windows.'

'OK,' I said. By this point I thought I should take a bit

of initiative instead of getting shoved around like a happy punchbag. Gripping Orla's hand, I led her out into a world that felt different, the way the world always does when you come out of the cinema after you've watched a good film. I never realised before that you get the effect even if you've hardly watched the film and you've run out before you get thrown out.

Or maybe, tonight, it was nothing to do with the film.

The sky was darkening to denim blue, the horizon dip-dyed a ghostly yellow where you could see it between shops and through closes. It was still warm; August was gone but it was shaping up to be one of those amazing, late-developing September summers.

'I could still get you a coffee,' I said hopefully.

'Nah.' She turned to me with a look that made my heart plummet into my intestines. 'I'd better go home.'

My lungs wouldn't work, my heart being lost in my guts and all. 'What d'you mean? Why? I thought we had all night?'

'Hardly,' she said with a roll of her eyes, but she must have seen the stricken look on my face because she said, 'Oh, give us a break. I mean, I just like to get home early. I'm going to my dad's at the weekend and Mum starts to panic, 'cause she hates having me out of her sight and everything. So I like to get home earlier the last few days. Before I go to Dad's, you know?'

'I thought I was going to see you at the weekend.'

'Well, you aren't.'

Shrugging, I let her go and stuffed my hands in my pockets. 'Fine.'

'Stop playing with yourself.' She pulled out my hand again and used it to tug me into a shop doorway. With a sinking sense of doom I saw we were opposite her bus stop. 'Look, I'm not making this up. I'll see you at school and I'll see you the week after.' She hesitated, not quite looking at me. 'If that's OK.'

Orla Mahon was asking me if it was OK. Hah! My heart surged up from my looping intestines and floated free. I ought to discuss my bizarre physiology with my Biology teacher.

'Yeah,' I said. 'Yeah, that'd be fine.' I was so relieved I remembered I wasn't the only human being in the world. 'How's your dad?'

'Fine. Sort of.' She put her arms around my neck and pressed her face against my skin. I felt her inhaling the smell of it, which made me very happy. Her warm breath sighed out against my neck. 'A year's such a long time but it isn't. There's a lot can happen in a year and you turn round and it's gone.'

I shivered. Years weren't supposed to spin by like that. I hated how my mind couldn't think of anything any more without thinking how soon I'd be dead and how fast it was all going to be over. I was seventeen, for God's sake. 'Why did he leave?' I blurted.

'Dad? 'Cause he had to.' She shrugged. 'Him and Mum couldn't live together any more. Aidan kept getting in the way. I think it started out that they kept going over all the things they could have done different so it wouldn't have happened. And then that changed a bit, so they were each wondering what the other could have done different. And I don't think they could get past that. I mean, once you thought it you wouldn't. Would you?'

I didn't say anything.

'And Mum didn't go to the trial. That didn't help. Especially with the way it went and all.' Pushing me away she tottered, folded her arms, looked at her watch, searched the road for her bus. 'I keep thinking all those things you always hear people say. You know? How he's never going to get married and he's never going to graduate and that. And I'm never going to have nieces and nephews and stuff. And my kids aren't going to have an uncle.' She stood on tiptoe and creased her eyes as if that would help her see the bus sooner. 'All those banal things.'

'It's only banal 'cause that's how it's meant to be,' I said. 'It's meant to be how things are. People are meant to do those things. And most people do and most people are good. Like, he was a good person.' A furious blush burned my cheekbones as Orla turned to examine my face.

'People always say that too, don't they?' she said. 'That's banal as well. But he was. He was a good person.'

I looked up for her bus. Not that I wanted it to come.

'I do want to see you again.' Unfolding her arms she rested them on my shoulders. Her fingertips touched the back of my skull, a light whisper of a touch.

'OK,' I said. I took her silver forelock between my thumb and forefinger and stroked it, because I'd been dying to do that all night.

She smiled and kissed me again. 'Here's my bus,' she said.

18

I don't know how I didn't notice what happened to Lola Nan. I was in a daze all week, torn between tormentingly unfulfilled bliss and the crashing comedown of the Orla-less weekend ahead. Of course I wasn't speaking to Dad and he wasn't speaking to me, but Mum could have told me. Whatever she said later, Mum could have found me and told me and I wouldn't have felt so bad about it or hated Mum so much.

By Friday I was dreading the weekend. For the first time I wished I'd taken that job shoving trolleys round the superstore car park, but I'd used the pressure-of-study excuse and it was hard to back down now. Anyway, I'd saved a reasonable amount of cash from my summer job and Dad, under duress, was still subsidising me. I went into town straight from school on Friday and bought a couple of CDs in a sale, thinking I could sync the most wrist-slitting tracks on to my iPod and mope around the park on Saturday. I was almost looking forward to it.

I called Mum, told her I wouldn't be home for tea, then pretended I'd lost the signal before she could make a fuss. All week Dad had worn a bitter look and a tight mouth, and there was a sourness to his breath each morning that signalled too many nightcaps and a truly filthy mood. I'd got to the point where I hated going home. Since that late-night scene with Dad, ironically enough, I'd just got angrier and angrier with Mum. I wished she'd stand up for me. I wished she'd forget Dad's feelings once in a while. I was starting to think it wasn't love and tenderness; I suspected she was scared of him and his silent tantrums. What was that expression of Orla's? Passive-aggressive. That was my dad. Passive. Aggressive. My PA.

The shops were open late and I hung around the HMV store looking at games and films and music till I was in a happy trance. I got to the point where I didn't care that the security guards were staring at me; I flicked through DVDs and CDs, the slap and click of the cases a hypnotic sound, and I made little bets with myself about which ones Orla would like. I wondered if she'd come home with me and watch them on the DVD player in my bedroom. When I pictured that, funnily enough, the scene in my head had us both fully clothed. I was propped against the headboard with her lying back against me, my arms round her waist and her head tilted back against my shoulder. I could almost feel the movement of her jaw around her gum as she stared at the screen. Involuntarily my muscles tightened, as if I already had her in my arms. The courtly-DVD-love scenario made my head float, then my body reasserted itself with a sick little shiver of lust.

I stared at the DVD case in my hand. I'd never even heard of this movie. I didn't know how I was going to last the weekend. I didn't even know when I was going to see her again. I was in love, I thought with a sudden shock. *Love,* as in real proper love. Oh, bollocks.

It was getting dark by the time I got home, and I paused outside the front door, swallowing, my throat tight and my pulse hammering. Well, I thought, a little foreboding was to be expected. Nothing good seemed to happen lately when I walked through this door. I wasn't having some horrible premonition; I was just psyching myself up for the silences.

Taking a breath, I stepped inside and shut the door. Allie was coming downstairs but she didn't smile at me. She stopped on the fourth step from the bottom and looked at me.

Actually, she looked right through me. Her pupils were huge, black and wide, and I hesitated, thinking for the umpteenth time how scary she could be. A few centuries ago they'd have burned her just for the look in her eyes. Next time she was asleep I'd check her scalp for the number of the beast.

The notion usually plastered a fond grin on my face. Not tonight it didn't. Allie gripped the banister, then sat down abruptly on the fourth stair. Tears glittered in her alarming eyes.

'I wish he wouldn't bleed,' she said.

There was that spider on my spine again, under the skin.

'What?' I said.

'He bleeds sometimes. I wish he wouldn't do that. It scares me.'

No dumping her, that's what I'd told him. I wished he'd dump her now, all right. 'Allie, don't talk like that.'

She shoved her hands into her hair and pushed it back behind her ears. 'I think it's when he's upset. He's upset tonight.'

'Stop it!' I yelled, flinging the little plastic bag of CDs at her. It bounced off the carpeted stair and her body jolted with shock. 'Stop it!'

She blinked, and I thought she was seeing me for the first time.

'Oh, Nick,' she said. 'Nick. I've got something awful to tell you.'

'Why didn't you tell me?' I said.

Mum glanced up. I'd found her where I expected, in what she called her office, though it was no more than a gap under the stairs with some modular Ikea office furniture fitted in like one of those clever-dick wooden brainteaser puzzles. She had the phone pressed to one ear, one hand resting lightly on her laptop keyboard. That hand lifted, palm outward, then she raised a single warning forefinger, putting me on hold. Her lips went on moving, talking into the handset, but I couldn't hear what she was saying for the high-pitched buzzing in my head.

'Why didn't *YOU TELL ME*?' I screamed.

Silence. The phone drifted away from Mum's ear. I could hear the questioning burble at the other end, but Mum just stared at me and didn't answer. Then she seemed to get her head together, and she muttered, 'I'll get back to you.'

The phone bleeped as she set it back in its cradle. 'Nick,' she said, but though her lips moved she didn't manage to say it out loud.

'You didn't say anything,' I said, more calmly.

'I didn't know how.'

'You should have thought of something.' Bitterness rose in my throat again.

'You must have known,' she said. 'You must have known we were thinking about it. We've talked about it.'

I just stared at her, and she averted her eyes, then looked back at me.

'It was all very sudden, Nick. A place came up in the home.'

'Somebody kicked the bucket, you mean.'

'A place came up,' she said again, 'and we had to make a decision.'

'This afternoon,' I said sarcastically.

'No, not this afternoon. Late last week. Do you think you've been approachable this week, Nick?'

'That's not my fault!'

'Your dad shouldn't have said those things to you that night, but how could he apologise? You've been gone since last week, Nick. You haven't been around. You don't come to breakfast. You don't come home for tea. How could we talk to you? How could your dad?'

Shoving my hand into my pocket, I tugged out my phone and brandished it in her face. Then I flung it to the laminate floor, where it clattered and broke, its metal skin splitting and flying off in two directions, each half spinning to a lazy circling halt.

She took a deep, shaky breath. 'I know you're angry. I understand. But we –'

'You could have looked for me,' I gritted through my teeth. I hated it when she did this. I hated it when she put on her professional face, when she was calm and reasonable, when she wanted to see all the sides. All sides but mine. That's the one she didn't want to see. If she saw that, none of us would end up being reasonable.

'You didn't want to be found, Nick! And how could I tell you something like this on the phone? How could I shout it out the door after you?'

Stop being so bloody clever, Mum. Stop it. The trouble was, I *had* been avoiding them all week. I knew she'd tried to talk to me because I remembered her saying a few times, as I shoved past her in the hall or the kitchen,

'*Nick I need to talk to you!*'

'Better than not being told at all!' I spat.

'Why would we? So you could argue and scream at us?'
I stared, silent.

'We couldn't cope any more,' she said.

'Oh.' I shouldn't say it, I shouldn't. But I couldn't help
myself. 'Did God give you a burden greater than you
could bear?'

There was a horrible silence. My face had warped into
a vile sneer but I couldn't seem to untwist it. Mum's
cheekbones reddened violently and she put up her hands,
scalded by the heat of her own shame.

'Don't throw that in my face, Nick. Please don't.'

'Don't start asking me for favours.'

'You didn't wash her sheets!' cried Mum suddenly. She
stood up, knocking the phone out of its cradle so that it
bleeped a protest. 'You never disinfected her cushion or
wiped her bottom. You never got called out by the police
because they'd found her wandering on the bypass. Do
you know how officials look at you? Do you? Do you
know how nurses treat you? Half your age and they treat
you like you're some feckless incompetent uncaring –'

'You never told me,' I interrupted coldly. 'You never
told me because you're cowards. That's the only reason.'

I thought saying it would make me feel better, but it
didn't. I felt grey and stony, and there was something
dying in my chest: a small wounded animal or maybe my
heart.

Mum sat down again, heavily. Her desk chair swivelled away from me, but she turned it back. 'Yes,' she agreed with a sigh. Glancing up at me, she smiled sadly. 'So you don't want to marry me any more.'

'Huh?'

'You used to tell me you'd marry me. When you were a little boy. All little boys say that to their mothers.'

'Do they?'

'All little boys start out the same, I suppose.'

I don't know if she meant that to sound so cruel. Did she actually mean it to sting the way it did? And I always thought she had such good intentions.

'I'm sorry about Lola Nan,' she said, as I kicked my heel into the carpet. 'Do you want to come and see her tomorrow?'

'No,' I said, viciously and truthfully.

I crouched to pick up the pieces of my phone. I didn't want to, it was humiliating, but I couldn't leave without it. My phone was my lifeline: it was my way to Orla and Orla was the only place I wanted to be. Kneeling beside me, Mum reached for half of the casing, but I shoved her hand away and snatched it up myself. I didn't look at her as I scrabbled to my feet, turned, and slammed out of the front door.

19

I put Lola Nan out of my mind. She was already out of her own; what could it hurt her to be put away like old china too fragile to be used any more? Best thing for her. Best thing for everyone. I put her out of my mind.

She barged back in at the worst of moments and the worst of places. I'd just come out of the sixth-year common room, fresh from a free period spent hiding W. H. Auden behind *V for Vendetta*, and I was on my way to Biology. I wasn't even thinking about Lola Nan, but about university and applications and whether the sciences were even my thing. I had enough qualifications for my second choice already and I wouldn't have stayed on for a sixth year if I hadn't wanted to keep an extra year's eye on Allie. And because I was afraid that as soon as I went away to university Lola Nan would take her sneaky opportunity and die on me . . .

I stopped dead. Somebody swore, having nearly tripped over me, and I got a deliberate whack from a swinging arm as he shoved past with the rest of the crowds.

'Feck's sake, move,' grumbled another voice behind me.

Ordinarily I'd have turned and given them my full Robert De Niro. *You talkin' to me? You talkin'a ME?* But I was frozen, my whole chest had seized up. Panicking, I looked from side to side.

McCluskey's office. How did I always end up here? The great Waiting Room of my life. I just knew that when I died and went to check in with the heavenly bureaucrats, I'd find myself standing outside McCluskey's office.

Nah. When people died they died. They turned into rot and putrefaction, and then they turned to dust. Then nothing. Not even a mind or a memory was left, and maybe that had been gone even while your lungs still breathed and your heart beat and your blood throbbed determinedly, pointlessly, round and round in your veins.

Nope. I definitely wasn't cut out for science, I thought, as I rapped violently on McCluskey's door and walked in without an invitation, then slammed the door and tried not to lean on it.

McCluskey looked up, and so did the second year he was berating. In the silence I stared at the open window behind McCluskey's right ear.

McCluskey stood up, reached past me to yank the door open once more and jerked his head at the shivering kid. 'Never do it again or you're dead.' He shut the door on him and sat back down at his desk. 'Right, Geddes, what is it?'

I squinted at the window. The sunlight was diffused through the branches of a weedy abused beech tree, but at this time of the afternoon the light was still strong enough for McCluskey to have half closed the vertical blinds. It striped McCluskey's desk with murky gold light. He reached up with his left hand and closed the blinds a little further, angling the light on to the council-issue calendar. September, Loch Lomond, The Bonny Banks Of.

'I have a problem, sir.'

'As do I, and its name is Geddes. What's yours?'

'I'm not immortal.' I stared at Loch Lomond.

'Aye. I'm waiting for the newsflash.' He jerked his thumb in what might have been an invitation. I sat down heavily in a hard little mustard-coloured armchair.

'They put her in a home,' I said.

He twirled his pen in his fingers, made marks on the paper. 'This is your grandmother.'

'Yeah,' I said.

'That's a shame. How's your sister?' he asked. Sketch, scribble.

'Mad,' I said.

'Well,' he said. 'That's a little awkward for everyone, isn't it?'

'You're telling me.' I scowled at the Bonny Banks.

'Your parents,' he said. 'They must be under a lot of pressure.'

'Oh yeah,' I said bitterly. 'Oh yeah.'

'You too, of course.'

There was something in my throat, something sharp and obstructive that stopped me swallowing. I thought about Lola Nan. Before and after.

'I just,' I said. 'I just sort of. I just sort of don't want to see her again.'

Scribble, scribble, sketch. He turned slightly, raised one eyebrow.

'Your grandmother, I take it. Not your sister.'

'Uh-huh.' I glowered.

'Joke, Geddes.'

'I don't want to go and see her,' I said, biting my lip. 'Maybe I think. Maybe I think she's better to just die now.'

'Uh-huh. That's understandable.'

'Are you taking the piss . . . Are you taking the mickey, sir?'

'No. Do try and realise you're not God, Geddes.'

'I thought that was your delusion, sir.'

'Ha ha.'

'I'm not trying to play God,' I said. 'I'm not going to put a pillow over her face or anything.' I blushed, seeing as it had fleetingly occurred to me.

'I never said you were. Stuff happens, Geddes. You can't stop it. It's not your fault.' His pen hovered in mid-air, and he growled, 'Not *always* your fault.'

'Oh, aye?'

'Oh, aye.' His turn to mimic me. It made my eyes burn.

'Know what? Everyone's breakable. Everyone's so fecking breakable.'

And then I burst into tears. Well, it wasn't that dramatic. I just felt my eyes fill, and when the lids couldn't hold any more the tears slid down my skin. I was horrified, mortified, but I couldn't stop them.

McCluskey let me cry for quite a long time, while he sat at his desk scribbling on his loose-leaf pad. When I blinked, rubbing my eyes with the flat of both hands until the paper swam in my vision, I noticed he was drawing clever little cartoon animals.

'OK, Geddes.' He set down his pen at last, closed the pad and stood up to pull on his jacket. Patting his pocket, he frowned and looked around his desk, till his eyes lit on a packet of mints. He stuffed them in his pocket. Still trying to quit, then. 'Miss your last class.' He glanced at his wall planner: council issue, teachers, for the use of. 'Biology, is it? I'll give Mrs Monaghan an excuse for you.'

Turning, he looked for a moment as if he'd like to put an avuncular hand on my shoulder. But he also looked as if he knew how much I'd hate that.

'You all right, Nick?'

I'd stopped crying by now. I stared at the ladder of sunlight across the window. 'Yes. Fine.'

'Well, you look like hell. Stay here till everyone's gone. Go out like that, you'll be dead in thirty seconds.'

'Thanks, Mr McCluskey.'

'OK. This too will pass, Geddes.'

He left me on my own then. After a few minutes my body unfroze and my eyesight cleared a bit more. I noticed his unwashed mug, stained with a ring of half-dried coffee at the bottom, and realised he wasn't that much of a control freak.

I really liked McCluskey a lot. For a bloody despot.

Every night for the rest of that week I left it till I knew Mum and Dad would be in bed, if not asleep – how could they sleep? – before going home. Mum would worry but I wanted her to worry. I called Orla, but I didn't get a chance to see her. Her mum had been frantic that night she came home so late – aye, that night *she* nearly drowned *me* – so Orla didn't like to go out again before she was due at her dad's. She was going to his place again this weekend, and I tried not to show my disappointment. She was going two weeks in a row because after that he was away for a month. Maybe I'd see plenty of her then. Meantime she went straight home from school and stayed in with her mum and her homework and some mutually agreeable DVDs.

When I closed the door on Friday night and stood in the hall, exhausted by late nights and walking, empty of anger, empty of everything but misery, the phone rang so abruptly and unexpectedly I couldn't for a moment think what the noise was.

Then I realised. I snatched up the handset before either

parent could have reached the one in their bedroom.

'Nick? Is that you, Nick?'

I'd known before I picked up, because who else would phone at this hour? But this was unexpected. She recognised me. She remembered me. The pain of my betrayal of her took my breath away.

'Nick?' she said again, and she sounded less certain of herself.

'Lola Nan,' I said. 'Yes. It's me.'

'I don't know where the fridge is!'

'Lola Nan, it's the middle of the night. Are you in trouble? Are you sick?'

'No.' Hesitation. 'I don't think I'm in trouble. Am I in trouble?'

'Lola Nan, listen. You have to call a . . .' Call a what? A nurse, a carer, a warden? What did they even call these people? I'd never asked. 'Call somebody. Is there an alarm?'

'A what? Where am I?'

'A cord or something. A button? Beside your bed. Please, Lola Nan . . .'

'I don't need a button! Why would I need a button?' Her voice grew sharper, with an undercurrent of whine. 'Boy! Is that you? Will you come and see me? I don't know what I'm doing here! I'm all alone! I haven't got anyone to talk to!'

'What about . . . what about Geoffrey, Lola Nan?' I bit my lip and shut my eyes tight, feeling cruel.

'Geoffrey's dead.' There were tears in her voice now. 'Geoffrey's dead.'

Oh, hell. So she hadn't been talking to Granda, only to herself. No imaginary friend for poor Lola Nan.

'I had someone to talk to at home. That nice boy. He doesn't come here, he doesn't come any more. Perhaps he can't find the way.'

'I'll come. Honest I will, I promise. Just go to sleep, Lola Nan. Go to sleep or call somebody.'

'What if he just can't find the way?'

I bit my lip harder. 'Please, Lola Nan. Go to bed. Go to sleep. I promise I'll come.'

There was a long silence that made my heart slow to a painful aching throb.

'All right. All right, boy. All right.'

My head swam with relief. Then I glanced up and saw with a sickening jolt that Dad was standing halfway down the stairs, staring at me. He was barefoot and he wore a pair of baggies and a thin misshapen Stone Roses T-shirt. His faded hair hung loose.

Swiftly I said, 'Bye now,' and hung up.

'Who was that?'

'Nobody,' I said. He must have appeared in the last few seconds. All the same, I don't know why I was lying.

He took a breath, angry red dots blossoming on his cheekbones, but I knew he was trying to be civil. His lips, pressed together, had dark wine stains in the creases. When he opened them I saw his tongue, dark red too with a stain his toothbrush hadn't shifted. 'Nick . . .'

'It was nobody,' I said again. 'Nobody you know.'

Frowning slightly, Dad shifted his eyes to my left, but I willed him to look at me and he did. There was bemusement as well as annoyance in his expression.

'Nick,' he said. 'Nick, your mother says I didn't listen to you the other night and I don't suppose I did and I wonder if we could . . .'

A phone interrupted him. For a horrible instant I thought it was Lola Nan calling back, and I knew I couldn't bear to talk to her in front of Dad. In fact I just couldn't bear to talk to her, not again. Luckily, it took only a fraction of a second to recognise my own ringtone.

It could only be one person. Tugging out my Sellotaped phone, I turned my back on Dad, facing the front door and the world beyond.

'Yeah, Orla,' I said.

After a little while I heard the stairs creak. Gazing into the pane of glass on the door, I saw his distorted reflection climbing slowly back up to his room. He didn't look back, and when he turned the corner at the landing I closed my eyes and leaned my forehead against the cool glass, giving myself an instant headache.

'Orla,' I said. 'I really need to see you.'

20

'So what changed?' I asked her.

She shrugged. 'My dad's work. He had to go away earlier than he thought. He cancelled.'

'He shouldn't have done that.'

Her fingers went lifeless in mine, and her voice cooled. 'My dad needs his work. It's important to him. Very important.'

Keep your mouth shut, Nick.

I squeezed her hand to make it mine again. 'Well, I'm glad anyway.'

When in a hole, Nick, stop digging.

'I'm glad you're still here,' I clarified. 'I'm glad I could see you.'

Why was it that around Orla I was lamer than a three-legged dog? But she said, 'Yeah. I know,' and her fingertips curled round the edge of my hand.

The early September sun was out, giving the grey sea a skin of light. We leaned on the chipped handrail watching the tide, which was right in, small dirty waves slapping the sea wall. A fag end, a plastic bottle and a piece of dirty orange rope rocked in the swell, sucked around in the motion of the water.

'Why is that?' said Orla.

'What?'

'Why is there always a bit of orange rope? When you go to the seaside there's always a bit of orange rope.'

'And half a tyre.'

'Yeah, that's right.' She scraped up a handful of small stones and started to use the bottle for target practice. 'And I dread to think what else.'

I thought, I went swimming in that. To impress this wumman, I went in there. Made my side itch just thinking about it.

'I'm glad you never let me drown.'

She gave me a sidelong look that was almost a smile. 'Me and all.'

I put my arm across her shoulders, happy when she leaned into me. A slight shiver ran across her skin, picked up and transmitted by my nerve endings. I liked this cooler weather.

'How's your sister?' Orla flung the rest of her gravel. It spattered on the water's surface and sank.

'Fine.' I was almost afraid to ask, in case she'd evaporated into small particles overnight, but I managed to say:

'How's your mum?'

'Kind of better.' Orla paused. 'She's at work. Works Saturdays.'

'I knew that.'

'She wanted to take the day off. Y'know, when Dad cancelled, she thought she should spend time with me instead. Said she felt guilty, but I told her not to be stupid. Like she has anything to feel guilty about.'

We watched the milky sheen of light undulate on the water.

'You know what she's really guilty about? Not coming to the trial. I talked to her yesterday.'

No comment, no comment, for God's sake. 'At least you and your dad were there.' And me and Mum, sitting one row behind and six chairs along. Even at the trial I could barely take my eyes off Orla.

'She should have been there from the start,' said Orla flatly. 'Couldn't face it, couldn't face Kev. I could see that, but it was wrong. No, not wrong, a bad decision. I kind of fell out with her yesterday, about that and . . . about Allie.'

'Did you?' I wasn't sure I wanted to hear this.

'I don't think Mum should give her a hard time. Because, you know, she's fine, Allie. Far as I'm concerned, if she needs my brother she can have him. Because of what she did.'

What she did.

Whispered the last words he'd ever hear and told him

he wasn't going to die? Held him in her arms as he died anyway? Lied to him? The last thing the boy ever heard was a lie.

Little white lie.

'Not that,' said Orla, like she could read my mind. 'The trial, I mean.'

What Allie did at the trial, then. And that was to look into Kev's eyes with her own dead black ones, make him look away, make him shiver and rub his neck and scowl. And then she looked at the judge and she said:

He meant to do it.

THEN

21

Kev said he didn't mean to do it. He panicked. It was an accident. He was defending himself, said Kev.

From the advocate depute's dark pessimistic scowl, I knew what she was thinking. She was thinking Kev was going to get off with culpable homicide and she was already seeing the tabloid headlines about his tiny wee sentence. She'd stopped making eye contact with Orla and her father, and I had a feeling that was a bad sign.

Mickey and his mother were in the front row, Mrs Naughton dabbing her eyes and occasionally blowing her nose. She looked gaunt and ill. Mickey, smart and well-groomed, frowned with concern for his mother. When he wasn't clasping her hand to his chest, he had his arm around her shoulder, squeezing her very, very gently as if she were made of delicate sentient crystal. Occasionally he threw troubled looks at his little brother, a picture of respectable concern. They were doing their damnedest to look like the kind of Good Family a boy like Kev might come from (aye, in a parallel universe). And they were succeeding spectacularly – in my view, in the advocate depute's, and quite obviously the jury's. There was one straggle-blonde middle-aged woman in the second row of the jury whose big blue eyes just about filled every time she looked at Kev. And she looked at Kev a lot.

You ask me, Orla was right. Mrs Mahon made a bad mistake not turning up that morning. She couldn't face the post-mortem evidence, and she couldn't be in the same room as her son's killer. But the trouble was, the only grief-stricken mother in the place was Kev's, and you could feel sympathy leaking her way from the jury. Some of them probably had teenage kids. (Straggle-Blonde undoubtedly did.) They knew how easy it was for them to get in trouble (ain't it just). They knew a boy could go bad just through the company he chose to keep (really). They knew some kids were stuck between a rock and a hard place. Felt threatened and scared. Lots of kids carried knives. Maybe theirs did too. A tragic case, but there but for the grace of God . . .

Kev wasn't stupid, either. He wasn't sullen or defiant or bolshie, he didn't spit or swear. Knowing Kev I bet he wanted to, but instead he looked hard at the front of the dock, blinking back tears and casting anxious glances at his mother, oozing guilt and remorse for what he was putting her through.

Allie helped him. Terrible, but true. I think she was overwhelmed, not by the courtroom but by her own responsibility. She wasn't used to justifying herself. She expected people to believe her: she'd always been believed, she didn't have to work at it. They must have thought she was a spoilt teenager who was used to getting her own way. By the end of her monosyllabic prosecution evidence, the advocate depute looked like she wanted to slap her.

It got worse with the cross-examination. She could hardly get her head round the concept. She couldn't understand why this defence guy wouldn't just take her word for it.

Kev's QC was called Urquhart and he was a nice-looking man. He was middle-aged, hair receding a bit at the temples, his voice resonant and pleasant. I liked him. So did the jury. I didn't much like the advocate depute. She looked permanently premenstrual.

'Alexandra,' said Mr Urquhart, in his nice voice. 'This must have been a terrible shock for you.'

Allie shot him a look of mild panic.

'After all, Kevin Naughton was your brother's good friend, wasn't he?'

'Um,' said Allie. 'I wouldn't say . . .'

'Wouldn't you? Really?'

'Well,' she said. 'Well. Yes. He was.'

'Except they fell out, didn't they? Not very long ago?'

'Um. Yes?' Allie's gaze flickered round the courtroom,

not landing anywhere.

'And some of Kevin's friends hurt your brother Nick?'

'Kev too,' said Allie. 'Kev was in on it –'

'Yes. Before that, Kevin and your brother were quite close friends? Hung around together?'

'Well, I . . . yes.' She shrugged. 'Suppose so.'

Sighing, Urquhart glanced down at his notes as if he'd lost interest. He stayed quiet for a while. Allie fidgeted.

'He was a big lad, Aidan Mahon, wasn't he?' said Urquhart. 'Played a lot of rugby.'

'Um,' said Allie.

'A little younger than Kevin, but very tall? Very well-built?'

'Yes,' said Allie. She pushed a strand of hair behind her ear. Her hand shook.

'He was the kind of boy who could and would defend himself. Wasn't he?'

'Yes.'

Allie looked at the advocate depute. The AD didn't look back at her. The jury watched both of them, and then their eyes swivelled one by one to Kev. He was blinking at the floor.

Lifting his head a little, Kev cast a pleading glance at Urquhart. As if he didn't want to blame Aidan for what had happened; as if things were already bad enough. Mickey squeezed Mrs Naughton's shoulders, then gave Kev a tiny grave nod of support. Kev looked back at the floor. Straggle-Blonde Juror's eyes filled again.

Smart boys.

'Of course, there's no question of this being the fault of Aidan Mahon,' Urquhart told Allie severely. (He never called him just 'Aidan'. He always called him 'Aidan Mahon'.) 'But it's easy for a young man to feel threatened, isn't it?'

'Yes.' She looked shifty.

'A teenage boy is more likely to be a victim of violent crime than a perpetrator. Isn't that true, Allie?'

'My Lord . . .' began the AD, waking up.

Urquhart shook his head. 'I apologise to my learned friend. But, Allie, do you think Kevin felt threatened by Aidan Mahon?'

'No,' said Allie, and took a breath to argue, but she never got the next word out.

'Scared.' Urquhart nodded. 'Is that unreasonable? Kevin thought Aidan Mahon had a knife. Haven't we all seen this often enough? Kevin's very *life* might have been at stake. Wouldn't he be scared? Wouldn't he lash out? Aidan Mahon came at him! This is what happens when boys carry knives, Alexandra. Fear. Panic. People get hurt. Even when –' he nodded at Kev – 'even when nobody means it to happen.'

Behind the dock's glass screen, Kev had his face in his hands. There was a suggestion of sniffling and snot, though I couldn't actually see his eyes. I was impressed. I'd have believed in Kev myself if I hadn't known him better.

When I saw Orla's pewter stare locked on the dock,

though, I decided that if anyone was capable of killing Kev, it wasn't Aidan: it was his big sister.

'Mickey said –' began Allie.

'Ah, Mickey!' Urquhart interrupted, and she shut up. '*You gonnae let him get away with that?* That's what you claim he said, Alexandra, yes?'

'Not *claim*, he –'

'*You gonnae let him get away with that?*' Shuffling his papers, Urquhart wrinkled his nose. 'It's all a bit Wild West, isn't it?'

'No, I don't –'

'And you are the only person, among all the many witnesses, who heard this alleged remark?'

'I . . . yes,' she said, and bit her lip.

He let that hang in the silence.

'Even if he said it –'

'My LORD!' snapped the AD.

'I apologise! I withdraw that. What you heard, it wasn't exactly an incitement to cold-blooded murder, was it? *Gonnae let him get away with that.* That could mean anything, couldn't it? And we only have your word for it, Allie.'

The AD didn't even bother to protest, though her little finger twitched. So did a muscle under her eye.

Urquhart studied Mickey and his mother. 'Michael was protective of his brother Kevin. Brothers and sisters: they look after each other. Don't you think so, Allie?'

Silence.

'It's natural and proper, isn't it? That's what families do. Your brother Nick looked after you, didn't he?'

She met his eyes. 'Yes.'

'And suppose your mother was very ill. Neither you nor Nick would want to cause her distress, would you? Do you think Kevin is very different from you? Do you think he's the kind of boy who would cause his sick mother needless distress?'

'My L—!'

'Yes, yes, withdrawn.' He hesitated. 'You're very close, you and your brother. Aren't you, Alexandra?'

That's when Allie stopped even looking at the QC. Instead, her dark eyes held the middle distance. Watching Aidan, probably. This was before we really knew what was happening with Allie; it was before the Aidan delusion had got too bad and obvious to ignore, but with hindsight that's what I think. She was watching Aidan and frankly she looked a bit deranged.

'I didn't mean to hurt you, Mum!' shouted Kev, slamming his palms against the dock's glass screen as his mother erupted into volcanic weeping. Mickey hugged her, rocked her in his arms. Kev's female solicitor soothed him, patting his arm – as she would – solicitously.

The judge sighed, and rolled his eyes, and looked at his watch, and stopped for lunch.

Staring round the courtroom I thought about the days after Aidan's death, the patch of power-washed pavement and the pile of stuff that got left on it. Flowers still smothered in cellophane, and home-made cards, some from people who'd hardly known him, with his smiling photo cut out of the paper. A rugby shirt, a rugby ball, teddy bears. *Teddy bears*, for God's sake. Maybe the display of belated affection was counterproductive, because if the jury thought of it at all, they probably imagined it was a gang thing. Teenagers sticking together. Teenagers being sentimental about a boy who'd been part of the whole threatening culture. We didn't even speak the same language, I realised, and I despaired.

Neither Orla nor her father had cried once. The Mahons' stiff upper lips were in danger of letting Kev get away with it, but I could hardly confront Orla in the corridors and tell her so. She was pretending I didn't exist, anyway. Outside the courtroom she was on her mobile for half an hour, mumbling remorselessly to God knew who, and she never once looked up.

When the courtroom was called to order again, Allie was recalled to the witness stand. And Mrs Mahon came in with her husband and Orla, and sat down in the front row.

Orla didn't put her arm round her mother, and Mrs Mahon didn't do any noisy crying, but the jury paid attention anyway. You couldn't mistake her manner for a stiff upper lip or emotional frigidity. It was grief-stricken dignity and it swathed her like a shroud she'd never shake off.

I swallowed and turned away, scared of seeing her cry

or crumble to nothing. Maybe Orla was wrong, maybe we all were; perhaps Mrs Mahon shouldn't have turned up at all. Bad enough that Allie's evidence was a disaster. Aidan's mother shouldn't have to sit through the whole sad farce.

Something had changed, though. Allie didn't look so intimidated now. She gave Urquhart a small direct smile, as if inviting him to go ahead and Make Her Day.

He did.

'Alexandra,' he began gently. 'I suggest to you that this wasn't Kevin's fault.'

Allie studied Kev, and then the jury, and then the judge. Her eyes were focused this time – they were dark and intent and frightening, but not mad.

'Kev meant to do it,' she said calmly.

Urquhart looked a teeny bit nonplussed. 'If Aidan had a knife . . .'

'But he didn't.'

'But Kevin *thought he did.*' The gentleness was leaking out of his voice, which was turning to sandpaper. 'And you were *behind* Aidan Mahon.'

'Yes. Because he stepped in front of me at the last moment.' She shrugged. 'He was trying to protect me.' She looked at the jury, not at me, and I felt my heart rip at the seams. 'That's what he did. That's what he was like.'

'I see. Would he have used a knife to protect you?'

She stared at Urquhart, who had gone puce at the ears, then glanced at Aidan's mother.

'Course he wouldn't. He never carried a knife.' When Urquhart tried to interrupt her she snapped, 'And I *could* see. Aidan had his hands up towards Kev. He was trying to stop him and the only thing he had in his hands was *my phone.*'

'Kevin could have mistaken that for –'

'Kev knew what it was. He'd just tried to take it off me. And he could see *fine.* We were walking away but Kev shouted at us. Aidan turned round to defend himself, to defend me. Kev pulled out his knife *after he saw Aidan didn't have one.*'

She paused, but Urquhart wasn't quick enough to interrupt.

'He knew Aidan wasn't armed. He could see that fine.' Allie stared straight into Kev's eyes. 'He wouldn't have gone for him otherwise.'

I think that's what did it. I think that, and the way Kev reddened and rubbed his collar and wriggled with fury. He looked like a kid caught out nicking sweets, like he was only sorry he'd been caught. He looked like the coward she was calling him. She was calm and brave and frightening, like a pale avenging ghost. The jury were watching Allie intently, and when they turned to Kev their eyes had chilled. Even Straggle-Blonde's.

Kev's fate turning on my sister's scary eyes. I was pleased, but it unnerved me.

Urquhart's shoulders hunched and he scratched behind his ear with a pen, glaring at his papers. The advocate depute was a lot less premenstrual now. She was down-right Mary Poppins. Hello sky, hello sun.

'To return to the beating given to your brother . . .' began Urquhart, then hesitated.

Allie looked at me at last. Her gaze was cool. 'That's my brother's business,' she said.

'So you didn't feel vindictive towards Kevin, even before Aidan's death? *Vengeful*? In your understandable grief and shock at this terrible event –' he was trying for a recovery there – 'you wouldn't decide to take revenge on Kevin for what happened to Nick?'

Allie never took her eyes off me. My collar felt tight. Orla had twisted in her seat, but my attention was locked on Allie.

Allie gave a small regretful shrug. 'Getting a kicking, that was Nick's fault for hanging out with Kev. He got what was coming to him. I think he knows that.'

I felt sick, my stomach lurching. Urquhart fidgeted, furious.

'So you tell us you wouldn't lie. Not to avenge your brother. Would you do it to avenge your boyfriend, Alexandra?'

She looked at Kev; she looked at the jury. She looked back at Kev.

'*I* don't lie,' she said.

The Mahons thanked her outside the court – well, through their solicitor they issued a statement that named Allie – but really she and Aidan's mother had done it between them. The jury had Allie's dark dead gaze burnt into the inside of their eyelids and that's what they must have remembered more than anything.

Premenstrual Poppy got her murder conviction; Kev got a life sentence. Well, I say 'life'. It never is, of course, but the judge set a tariff of twelve years. That's quite severe. So I'm told.

Still, all Mrs Mahon had to do for her part was turn up. Allie had to perform in front of the whole courtroom, and worse, she had to walk past Mickey and his weeping mother as we left. And he didn't have to act any more.

He let go of his mother as he swung to face Allie, blocking her way, his thin good-looking face twisted into an ugly mask. I shoved forward but he ignored me and he didn't touch my sister. He wasn't stupid. He wouldn't touch her.

Not now, anyway.

Allie met his deep-set brown eyes as the corner of his mouth curled up.

'I never forget a face,' he said. 'Bitch.'

NOW

22

I could still picture Mickey's twisted leer, his implied promise. Mickey wasn't in jail. I shivered.

He'd never dared come after Allie before now. I'd always known he wouldn't. His little brother was serving a life sentence and his mother's grief was genuine, if noisy. He wouldn't lose her another son.

Not while she was alive.

I shivered again.

Poor woman. Never killed anyone. So sad.

She wasn't alive. The trial hadn't killed her but she was dead. She didn't have feelings to hurt any more. The cancer came back. With a vengeance.

That can be fatal, you know. Stupidhead.

She wasn't there to be damaged. Unlike –

No, no, no. Mickey was spit and wind and empty threat, and I couldn't live with any other possibility, because what could I ever do about it otherwise? It wasn't enough to take to the police: one name-calling and a parking incident on a public road.

I never forget a face. Bitch.

So what? Face recognition. Not an uncommon talent.

They'd laugh at me. I'd seen these things in the papers, in the TV news. The police had other things to think about; they had targets to meet. And if I asked Dad to tell them he'd get purple and high-pitched and high-dudgeoned. They'd laugh even more at Dad.

What was I supposed to do to protect Allie? You have to look after yourself.

I shook my head violently. Orla was still leaning on the rail cemented into the sea wall, gazing down, cool as the gunmetal sea. Just watching her made me feel better.

Something struck me then. It just sort of fell off my tongue and out of my mouth.

'You're so strong,' I said. 'I can't take any more brittle people. You touch them and they break.'

Orla turned. For a moment she examined my face, then she reached out and drew one fingertip along the straight line of my eyebrow.

'I won't break.'

'No,' I said.

She glanced out to the horizon. 'I need to go home now.'

'Why?' I was bitterly and abruptly disappointed. 'I thought your mum was at work.'

She eased away from my arm, took her gum from her mouth between thumb and forefinger, and dropped it into the sloshing grey waves.

'Come back with me,' she said.

23

When I used to fantasise about kissing Orla Mahon, I'd imagine her being taller than me. I knew she wasn't, even in heels, but I used to picture myself standing on tiptoe to reach her mouth. Maybe it was because I felt so intimidated. Fortunately it wasn't like that in real life; I was a good few centimetres taller than she was.

Vertically, anyway. Horizontally speaking, we fitted together perfectly.

It didn't go like my fantasies. Nothing wild or crazy about it. She moved with me like an extension of my own body, warm and intense and electrifying. I felt it everywhere: in my bones and up my spine and into my fingertips. It jolted and tore me like I'd never be in one piece again, and I know she felt the same thing, because there was a moment there when we were the exact same person.

Afterwards I propped myself above her on my fists and stared into her tarnished-pewter, North-Sea-in-winter eyes. I was afraid of opening my mouth in case I came over all James Blunt, so I pressed my lips together and tried not to say anything.

I didn't want to look at the clock in case the hands had moved too fast. I didn't want to leave her rumpled single bed, didn't want to move my rigid arms from either side of her because I wanted to keep her there for ever. Not that she tried to escape. She placed both her palms against my face and gazed up at me, calm and intent. I inclined my head one way, then the other, aching after her touch like a loyal dog, loving the light scratch of her black-red fingernails against my ears. I felt pathetically grateful, like a stray who'd found a home, but she didn't look superior. She looked as if she'd found a missing piece too. Another ripple went through her body, and I shuddered in echo. I wished I didn't have to leave. I thought about the parallel world I had to go back to, and I shivered again, and Orla's hands tightened on my face. She smiled, her hands sliding down my face and to the back of my neck. Gently she pulled me down beside her.

I lay on my side, my arm possessively across her torso, my fingers curled round her upper arm, testing the texture of muscle where her soft skin slid across it. She gazed at the ceiling, a tiny smile tugging the corner of her mouth.

'So,' I said, 'will you still respect me in the morning?'

She gave a small inelegant snort.

'You do bring out the lame git in me,' I added.

'I know.' The dent of her smile deepened, then turned to a thoughtful frown. 'Maybe I should call the baby Aidan. Mum would be mad to start with, but in the end she'd be happy. What d'you think?'

God Almighty. That turned my spine cold, for more than one reason. 'Er,' I said.

The frown vanished as she laughed and rolled over to face me. It was a lovely sound. 'Oh, breathe, you daft git. It'd be stupid, that's what.'

I laughed too, like a gasp of relief.

'So, careful with the condoms,' she added. 'Don't open the next one with your teeth.'

The next one. I touched her nose ring and kissed her. 'Sorry. Bit of a hurry. Stupid as well as ugly.'

'You talkin' a *me*?'

'No,' I said, 'you daft git.'

God, could she get any more perfect? She could quote *Taxi Driver*.

Her wicked grin faded as she examined my face. She touched a fingertip to the side of my broken nose. 'You're not ugly,' she said casually.

There was nothing casual in the way her finger traced my brow, and the dip of my temple, and the hard line of my jaw, then came to rest in the hollow of my throat. She must have felt me swallow hard; I felt her fingertip rise and fall. I thought about the other bedroom, the one next to this one, the one she hadn't glanced at as she gripped my hand tighter and pulled me past. The door had been slightly ajar but *Don't look*, she'd said. *It's like he's still there.*

I thought about Mrs Mahon going in and lying on his bed and holding his clothes and crying. I thought about Orla lying here listening to that, and then having to put up with my sister, pretending. *It's like he's still there.*

It was, sort of. I didn't feel threatened, though, or angry. If Aidan was around, he didn't scare me. It wasn't about him. Not this.

Later in the afternoon Orla fell asleep, but I didn't. Through the thin curtains a low afternoon sunlight filtered. Divided by the window frame, it split in one rhombus in the centre of the carpet and one on the duvet cover. I lay and watched the dancing light, wondering what was making it move, and then I focused on the dust motes that swirled and circled, rose and sank, never falling: plane after plane of them. Galaxies, nebulas, constellations of them. Staring into them, I searched for suns and planets. I wondered if I was an atom of a dust mote in a bar of light in someone else's dimension, some other lucky bastard's bedroom.

Then I watched the dusty light fall across Orla's skin and hair, glint off the silver ring in her nostril, and I didn't care any more. My arm tingled, numb where she lay on it, but I didn't want to move. I let her breath touch the skin inside my elbow and didn't care if my arm fell off, or if my planet, my whole universe, was grit on someone's cosmic shoe. I loved Orla Mahon, and there was a reasonable chance that she loved me back. Which was fine. That was all it took.

I thought, it'll be all right now.

Oh, right.

24

I should have got Orla out of my system, now that I'd actually slept with her, but sometimes I thought I was going to spend the rest of my life in a hazy Orla-dream. That's where I was the next afternoon: on my back in a colder, emptier bed, trying to remember the touch of her fingertip on my eyebrow. How her skin tasted. How cool or warm her breath was when it touched different parts of my flesh. It was a lot to remember; it took a lot of my concentration. I'd already switched off my phone, because Orla never called me when she was spending quality shopping time with her mother, and there was nobody else I wanted to talk to. Now I closed my eyes and swore violently, trying to ignore the insistent ringing of the doorbell.

'No Words of Wisdom today,' I muttered at the ceiling. 'We're out of stock.'

Ring, ring. Hammer hammer hammer. Ring.

'Nobody home. The Soul Doctor is Out.'

Hammer. Riiiing. *Riiiiiiing.*

'Eff off and get a life.'

Riiiiiiiiiiiiiiiiiiiiiiing.

I thought this was what parents were for. Answering the door.

Course, they were both out. Seemed like they disliked my company as much as I disliked theirs. Growling, I rolled off the bed and slouched downstairs. If this was the Jehovah's Witnesses, there was about to be a Crime of Religious Hatred.

That could not be a familiar silhouette beyond the distorting glass. It could *not*.

I flipped the snib and flung open the door. Oh yes, it could.

'You're dead,' I told Shuggie.

He didn't look intimidated, of course, but it struck me that he wasn't wearing his usual calmly critical, lost-in-space look. He was panting, chest heaving, his eyes wide and scared.

'It's K-Kev,' he said.

'What?'

'I . . . I've seen . . .' He hauled in a breath, stammered something incoherent, all consonants. At last he managed, 'I seen him!'

That was something I never thought I'd witness: Shuggie losing his grasp of English grammar. 'You can't have seen Kev, Shugs. He's in the slammer.'

Getting his breath and his brain back, he shook his head violently, as if it was me that was being stupid. 'No, *no*. Not Kev. Kev got stabbed.'

'*What?*' Shuggie really brought out the drooling idiot in me.

'In the Young Off— . . . in that place. He got in a fight. Got in a fight and got stabbed.'

'*How could he get stabbed?*' I roared.

'Sharpened spoon.' Shuggie blinked, as if he was thinking. 'You can sharpen the –'

'Shut up! You can't have seen him! Where did you see him? Hospital?'

'No, no, I didn't see *Kev*. Mickey. It was Mickey I saw.'

'*What?*'

'Stop saying that!' cried Shuggie. 'It was Mickey, understand? I saw Mickey. He's raving, off his head, cursing Allie to hell and back. It's Mickey I saw!'

I was only immobile for a moment. Then I spun and ran back into the house, taking the stairs two and three at a time, grabbing the banister and hurtling round the landing so fast I almost stumbled. In my room I yanked on the drawer so hard it shot right out of the wardrobe. I fell on my backside, then scrambled up to dig among the jumpers. Shuggie stood at my back.

'When?' I snapped. 'When did you see him?'

'Hour ago.'

'Where've you been?' Unfair and savage, but I couldn't

help it. Why didn't the little tosser have a phone?

'Your phone's off. I tried to phone you, I borrowed one.'

I snatched my phone out of my pocket and stared at it stupidly.

'Did you call the polis?'

'I never thought. I was trying to find you. I never thought . . .'

He was babbling. I wished he'd shut up. I wished I didn't own so many damn jumpers. 'Shut up. You did right. Shut up.'

'I looked everywhere, Nick.' He was almost in tears. 'Never thought you'd be home.'

I didn't reply. Fair enough.

Even his voice sounded white. 'Mickey won't hurt her.'

'Yes he will.' I couldn't find the bloody knife, couldn't find it. I flung jumpers aside. Catching one reflexively, Shuggie clutched it against his chest.

'He wouldn't dare, Nick, he wouldn't.'

'Yes he would.' I didn't know why I was wasting my breath. Shuggie knew he was talking crap; he was only trying to calm me down. Oh God, *there*, at last. I snatched the knife from a fold of sweatshirt fabric. Even through scraps of *Daily Record* I cut my finger, but I didn't have time to suck it. Shuggie stepped hurriedly out of my way as I grabbed my jacket.

'Get the polis,' I said.

I think he tried to follow me because I heard him shouting my name, but he couldn't keep up. Just as well. He'd done his bit and I wouldn't want him keeping up, not now. Good old Shuggie. Time to butt out of my business now.

I was thumbing my phone keypad as I ran, but remembered in two-and-a-quarter seconds there was no point. Allie's phone had been nicked. She hadn't got a new one yet. *Didn't like it. Never used it.*

I was keen not to fall, there being a blade shoved into my pocket, but I ran as fast as I could anyway. After a bit I slowed to a jog. After all, I didn't know where she was.

My lungs hurt. Hesitating at the pedestrian traffic lights by a huge roundabout on the bypass, I felt panic choke me. I didn't know where to start. I thought about the High Street, and the shops. If she was in town, she'd be safer. Mickey wasn't stupid enough to attack her in front of loads of people, and even if he was, someone would intervene.

I thought about that for a moment. No, they wouldn't.

Then I remembered Drugstore Cowboy, and Richie the not-very-bright security guard. Richie was hard enough, or he thought he was. Richie was willing to have a go at me, and he was big and ugly enough to have a go at Mickey. Please, Allie, I thought. Please be shoplifting in Drugstore Cowboy. Even if you get arrested for it, please be busy nicking stuff. In fact, please get arrested and taken to the cells. Best place for you.

The little green man bleeped at me. I stood and stared at the crossing. Cars had had to stop for the red light and one driver was mouthing abuse at me and tapping his temple. Then he tapped it harder, called me a name I could lip-read. I could only stare at him. As soon as the lights started flashing he screeched away with a stink of scorched tyres.

I didn't know what to do. Turning one way, then the other, I whimpered.

A bunch of girls came to a halt across the road from me, poking their fingers into bags of hot chips, laughing and swearing when they got burnt. They didn't wait for the green man, just sauntered across, earning blasts of horn from drivers and repaying them with a finger and a mouthful of shrieked abuse.

'Oy, gorgeous.' One of them grinned at me through the chip clamped between her teeth like a cigarette. She had a scraped blonde ponytail, smoky made-up eyes, a row of gold studs edging her ear like glittering bites. She reeked of chips, heady and vinegary.

'Gina,' I said. I was acceptable in the sight of Orla's gang now, but a fat lot of use they were to me. Hopelessly I said, 'You seen my sister?'

She swallowed the chip, screamed abuse at a lorry driver, then turned back, shrugging.

'Lost the heidcase again? Can you not tag her or something?'

'Forget it,' I spat, and turned to make for the railway bridge.

'Oy,' she shouted after me.

I didn't have time for Gina to take the piss and I spun on my heel to tell her so, but she wasn't laughing, she was frowning. She nibbled the end of a chip, then pointed it at me.

'Second person that's asked me that.'

25

She went thataway. Just like a bad old western. *Thataway.*

Twenty minutes. How far could Allie have got in twenty minutes? Could Mickey have got to her in ten? Had Gina even remembered those timings right?

Course I didn't tell Mickey where to find her. I just said, she went thataway, and he said, Oh yeah, she goes down that field by the tracks, by that old caravan, doesn't she? And I said, Yeah, 'cause he obviously knew fine. Said he had a message for her. That's all.

Bloody, bloody, thoughtless Gina. Why did she tell him? Dapper Mickey, charming Mickey, psycho Mickey.

But she told me too. Lovely, lovely Gina.

No time to fall silent and wait for the train song, though I knew it must be almost time for the fast train to come through. I took one glance down the line, made out that the level-crossing barriers were still raised, and ran down the embankment, my heels jamming into the slope and jarring my knees. I didn't pray or anything, I just said in my head *Please* as I jumped down and ran on to the tracks. As I crossed the first rail, believe it or not, I shut my eyes, and I kept them shut all the way. So much for tripping on rails or catching my foot in a sleeper. I could do this with my eyes shut and I'd proved it. *Hah.*

I almost fell on to the opposite embankment, then scrambled up it, clutching handfuls of weed and nettle and dead willowherb that broke when I put my weight on it. I don't think I stung my hands. Anyway, I was too busy praying that Mickey had taken the long way round.

What kind of sentence would I get? What if I didn't kill him? What if I just hurt him, not too much, mind, just enough to let Allie get away? I didn't want to hurt anybody but I kept thinking about Mickey kicking the crap out of Kev, snapping Kev's skull on to his knee, half killing the wee bugger. And he *loved* Kev.

This was bad. This was very bad. I ran, my lungs cramped with pain.

At the top of the slope I stopped, gasping in air that hurt my chest. *There.* She was sitting cross-legged against a tree by the grubby burn, a magazine open in her lap, a can of Coke at her lips. Swamped with relief, I watched her lower the can to the ground, wriggle it into the dent she'd made for it in the soft earth, and flick over a page of the magazine.

I opened my mouth to call to her, but no sound came out, because that's when I saw Mickey.

He was coming from the other direction. Of course he hadn't gone on foot. What had I been thinking? He'd picked up his car from wherever he'd parked it, and he'd come by the back country road. He knew those little roads. Obviously he'd made it his business to know Allie's favourite spots, too. He must have spied on her, long before he'd summoned up the nerve and the guts and the pure volcanic rage to do something about her. And now he had, and now he was walking swiftly towards her from the opposite direction. I could see the bonnet of the blue Mondeo, parked beyond the broken-down wire fence.

I ran again, pelting down the slope and across the field.

I don't know if Mickey saw me but he had a good head start and he was too cool to run. Too cool and too certain. I never knew this ground was so uneven. How could I not have noticed that before? I kept stumbling and tripping, and once I sprawled in a patch of bog and felt the shape of the knife dig into me, reminding me. Hell, that was close. I clambered to my feet, pulling out the knife and tearing the newspaper clumsily off it as I ran.

Allie stood up. She'd seen Mickey now, and she looked back and saw me too. She hesitated for an instant, then she was half walking, half jogging towards me, glancing back over her shoulder at Mickey. She looked uncertain, as if she couldn't quite believe she ought to run.

Believe it! I thought. *Just run anyway, Allie!* But I didn't have breath to spare to yell it.

I'd cut my hands but at least I had a good grip now on a naked knife. Which was just as well, because Mickey was running now too, sure-footed, fast and confident. When Allie reached me and I grabbed her arm and swung her behind me, he was only a few metres away.

My breath sounded terribly loud and high-pitched. I sounded terrified, I realised, and maybe that's why Mickey had that big fat smile on his face. I raised the knife warningly.

'Leave her alone,' I managed to say.

'Who's gonnae make me?' he hissed.

I swallowed. 'I'm sorry about Kev but it's not her fault.'

I was pushing Allie back, trying to get her to go further away, but her fingers still gripped the hem of my shirt. The ground was more treacherous than ever when you were walking backwards. Mickey just kept coming on as we inched back towards the slope and the cutting. We were going to be cornered, I realised. If we got that far, I wasn't walking backwards across the rails. No way. The fast train was due. I'd rather take my chances with Mickey.

When we were almost at the foot of the slope I shook Allie off and shoved her away, heard her take a few more steps. Why didn't she just run? I couldn't take my eyes off Mickey.

'Bugger off, Allie!' I yelled.

She moved back a little more. I could see her in my peripheral vision and I could still hear her breathing. She could go now, run, flag down a car at the level crossing. Why didn't she? I gripped the knife tighter, because my palms were sweating and the handle felt slippery.

'Go,' I shouted.

Mickey took a step forward, and I lashed at him.

Another. I lashed out again. And again, slashing downwards, but his hand was waiting and he caught my arm. He grinned.

Damn, he was strong.

Then we were scrabbling, whacking, grunting together, wrestling on our feet like a pair of girls. Nothing cool or martial-arty about it, I can tell you. He was stronger than me, wrenching my arm up and behind me, and while I clawed furiously at his face he snapped the knife out of my hand, and stumbled back.

He took a step towards me, my confiscated knife in his fist. I took a step backwards, and so did Allie behind me.

'Get lost, Allie,' I said, and this time I heard her move further away.

Mickey's eyes followed her, then flicked back to me. There were tears in them.

'My wee brother's in a coma,' he spat. 'Because of *her*!'

I said, 'Your wee brother's in a coma because of you.'

There was a moment of silence. Just long enough for me to be amazed that you could commit suicide with nothing more than your foot and your own big mouth.

Then Mickey roared, and punched me in the gut.

Oh, he hit me hard. It took my breath right away. I doubled over, stumbled on to my knees, clutching my belly. With half my mind I was aware of Allie running at last, scrambling up the slope, running as fast as she could away from Mickey and me. That was good. About time.

The other half of me was thinking: What's with all the blood?

Mickey was still standing over me, breathing hard, as I stared at my bloody hands. I didn't want to move them away from my belly. I didn't want to look away from them and the blood seeping down over them, but out of the corner of my eye I saw my knife at his side, held with a light expert confidence. The blade of that was all bloody, too.

'You stupid wee tosser,' I heard him say, and he gave a brief barking laugh. 'That wis definitely self-defence.'

He turned on his heel and ran up the slope after Allie, so obviously the thing to do was to get to my feet and follow him. So I did, except I managed one step and I was on my knees again.

But if I didn't follow, he was going to kill Allie.

But if I did follow, there was going to be more blood coming out of the hole I could feel under my fingers. I gave a sob.

I stood up again and this time I managed five steps before I was on my knees. Which was when I realised, with my usual quick-thinking brilliance, that I was not going to catch them up. I tried to howl with rage but what came out was a pathetic keening sound.

I was going to have to let go of my belly and grab the weeds and get up that way. I did that, with one hand, though I was still scared to move the other one that was holding me together. Oh God, I thought, and I loved Orla Mahon, all the way, and now I was going to die.

When I got to the top of the embankment I crouched there on all fours. Well, three of my fours, since one hand was still holding in my blood, and not doing a terribly good job of it. I peered one way and then the other, moaning with despair as I caught sight of them. Allie was running now, really running, but not towards the level crossing; she was pelting up the left-hand side of the tracks towards the tunnel. What was she thinking? She probably wasn't thinking at all. She couldn't, mustn't go in the tunnel, and she wouldn't cross the tracks. I knew she wouldn't. I knew that because the train was singing.

I had no breath to scream at her, but I was yelling in my head, *Stop stop don't don't Allie no.*

She hesitated, glanced over her shoulder at Mickey. He was no more than five metres behind her and he'd slowed his pace, moving my knife from one hand to the other. I couldn't see his grin but I could imagine it. Allie looked terrified now, backing away, wildly looking for a place to run. Then her head jerked round, and she ran. Right across the tracks.

The song was louder, buzzing in my head as she ran,

and I couldn't breathe because I just knew she was going to catch her foot. But she didn't. She leaped delicately between the rails to the other side.

I thought she'd scramble up the embankment now, but she didn't. She stayed in the cutting by the tunnel mouth, and turned and looked straight at Mickey.

Mickey hesitated just the once. Then he ran. Perhaps he couldn't hear the song; perhaps he just thought he had time.

Actually he probably did have time. I couldn't believe Allie wasn't running, couldn't believe she would just stand there and lock her black solemn eyes on Mickey as he ran. *Run run Allie go go run.*

Boy, I'd changed my tune, but it didn't make any difference. She simply gazed at him, arms straight and hands fisted by her sides. And Mickey stopped.

I knew Allie was scary sometimes but I thought that was just me. Sure, Mickey can't have expected her to stand there and stare him down. All the same, I don't know why he'd be goggling at her like that, then backing off a step, my knife falling out of his limp fingers.

Why did he stop? He'd have made it if he hadn't stopped. But the roaring song and the tremor of the tracks must have confused him, because he looked down at his feet in stupid fear.

He was there and then he wasn't. Was-not-there. The train was there: for one second, two seconds, three seconds. The flash of lit windows, a child on its mother's lap, swaying businessmen, bums against the seats, *Daily Telegraph* in their hands. That was it: gone.

It must have been starting to stop; it would, wouldn't it? It must have jolted as the driver braked, and some of the businessmen probably stumbled and cursed. Nobody realises how fast they go. You blink and they're there, you blink and they're gone. It would have been braking, but it was already gone.

I didn't watch Mickey die; he was moving too fast for the eye to see. He died at such a speed, and besides, my vision was misty. Far up the tracks, towards the level crossing, the train was finally drawing to a halt.

I didn't want to look down at the rails in case he was there. I don't think he was, I think he'd been carried further up the track and he was somewhere under the train, maybe in more than one place, but I didn't want to look. So I looked across the cutting, desperately searching for Allie, but I was finding it so hard to see. My eyes kept blurring.

When I focused at last, there was someone with her on the far side of the line. A boy about Allie's age, a boy with fair hair spiking out over his forehead. She didn't speak to him – still too shocked, maybe – and after a moment he turned to walk away. I blinked again, squeezing sweat out of my eyes, and could hardly get my eyelids back open, but when I did, he was gone.

Didn't want to get involved, I guess.

26

'I'm sorry,' said Allie. 'I'm sorry I ran away and left you.'

I gave her a filthy look. 'What d'you mean, sorry? I wondered what took you so long. Couldn't you take a hint?'

She plucked another grape, and when I shook my head she ate it herself. She had eaten virtually the whole bunch, together with the chocolate supply brought by Shuggie.

'I didn't want to leave you,' she added, 'but he made me. He told me I had to.'

I clenched my teeth. I didn't have to ask who had persuaded her to run: not Mickey, that was for sure. Well, for once her delusions had come in handy. 'Can you not sit on a chair?'

'Comfier here.' She patted the mattress, then my hand, lifting it to examine the hospital bracelet. Bored of that, she reached for my notes. 'Says here you have a month to live. D'you want Robbie Williams as they're carrying you out, or is that a bit of a cliché?'

'Ha fecking ha,' I said.

'Sorry.' She gave me a smile, her eyes brown and sparky behind her blunt fringe. You wouldn't think they could turn so scary and black.

'Allie,' I said. 'Why did you stop?'

'I didn't stop.' She laughed, light and gurgling. 'Mickey stopped.'

There was a note of satisfaction in her voice that made me shiver. I remembered her saying that about Aidan. *He stopped.* And now Mickey had, too.

I pressed her. 'You stopped after you crossed the tracks. That was stupid, Allie.'

'Well, Aidan told me to. I hated leaving you but he –'

'Allie . . .' I said. There was a chill at the base of my spine.

'He knew it would be OK.'

'How? How did he?' My voice rasped, growing higher-pitched. 'What if he'd told you to stop on the tracks?'

'He wouldn't do that,' she said kindly. 'And he knew what to do and he knew it would be fine. Because Mickey said it himself.'

I stared at her.

'Mickey said so, remember?' she told me. 'He never forgot a face.'

'Don't,' I shouted. The man in the opposite bed shook

out his paper and glared at me. 'Don't,' I whispered. My voice shook. 'Don't say that. Don't say any more.'

It was too much delusion, or it was Allie at her most manipulative. I wouldn't ask her again; I didn't want to hear any more of this. But how had she made Mickey stop? Just by doing what he least expected? Just with the dead glare of her frightening eyes? Yes. Yes. Because there wasn't any other reason he would stop. There just wasn't.

Even if he never forgot a face.

She looked at me, and nodded kindly. She didn't say it.

'Kev's recovering. Did you hear? He came out of the coma.'

'Yeah,' I said. 'I'm glad.'

'Believe it or not?' She smiled. 'Me too.'

I fiddled with my hospital bracelet, which was making my wrist itch. 'Dad came earlier,' I told her. '*Again.*'

'I know. You're the next thing to Mahatma Gandhi, you know. You're JFK meets Nelson Mandela. You're the Prodigal Saint, I haven't got a look-in. He's back home slaughtering the fatted lentils.'

I grinned. 'God help me. See that horrible smell? That's the food. Can you sneak me in a cheeseburger?'

'I'll bring you anything you want,' she said seriously.

'Orla Mahon,' I said.

She looked at me sadly. Allie knew fine Orla hadn't been to see me. Not once.

I loved her, all the way. I remembered thinking that when I thought I was going to die. I loved her all the way in to my bone marrow and beyond, and I'd only not-slept with her once, and I'd wanted to do it for ever. Leaking life into the weeds by the tracks it had seemed like the biggest regret of my foreclosed life. I didn't want co-star billing any more. I didn't want to be Kev-shaped or, God help me, Mickey-shaped. I didn't want to be a boy who carried a knife. I wanted to be a boy who pissed off his girlfriend by talking through a film.

Six weeks I'd been watching the grumpy old bugger in the opposite bed read his paper. Six weeks I'd been stuck here waiting for her, bored out of my skull, lovesick to my wounded innards. I wanted to see Orla more than I wanted my own mother, but she hadn't been near the place. She hadn't been near me. I guess that was that, then.

Thinking about Orla actually made me wince with pain, and Allie bit her lip anxiously. She glanced at my belly. 'Does it still hurt?'

'Terrible,' I said. I was planning to milk this for as long as I could. 'No Robbie Williams, get that?'

She laughed and stroked my hand. 'Oh, Nick, don't worry. You're going to live to be such an old fart.'

'Oh, yeah?'

'Yeah. Believe me, I know. I just know.'

For some bizarre reason I did believe her. 'So, Mystic Mentalcase. Am I going to get any more shagging with Orla?'

If I didn't have a laugh, you see, I was going to cry, but

Allie shook her head reproachfully. 'What d'you take me for? Psychic or something?'

'Yeah,' I said.

'Well.' She tapped her nose as she slid off the bed and stood up. 'There's limits. I'm not a frigging hypnotist.'

'I'm bored,' I whinged, desperate to keep her with me.

'You're getting out soon. And I'll come again tomorrow. It's Saturday.' She hesitated. 'Nick?'

'Uh-huh.'

'He's gone now, Nick.'

'Oh. Has he?'

'He's not coming back,' she said. 'This time he really isn't.'

I wanted to believe her. I so did.

27

'Hey, Lola Nan.' I kissed her withered cheek.

She gazed at me blankly. I expected her hand to tap thin air, but it didn't. She sat very still, looking so terribly lost a bolt of guilt went through my stomach. That hurt, I can tell you. I gritted my teeth, and made the grimace into a sort of smile. She wouldn't know the difference.

At least she had her own room. There were sepia pictures of Granda in an army uniform, and an old primary school picture of me and Allie, Allie solemn and dark, me scowling, my arms round my sister. Not the best picture we ever had taken but probably the age she best remembered us at. Mum thinks of things like that.

The place smelt of cabbage and pee and Dettol. It reminded me of the hospital, and I found it unsettling, but Lola Nan didn't look unhappy. The floor was lino, streaky-patterned like blue bacon, and the bed was all white sheets and metal bars, except for the pink fluffy hot-water bottle we'd bought her last Christmas. There was a red alarm cord. Several, actually: one by the bed, one by the basin, one near the shiny PVC armchair. I wondered if she'd ever have her head together enough to pull any of them. I peered out of the window. Below me was a patch of grass and a flowerbed that had been emptied for the winter, bare and loamy. Between the gables of the roof you could see quite a lot of sky.

I sat down beside her, laid my hand on her chair arm. Smiling sideways at me, she rested her hand on mine, then began to pat it, rhythmically. I stared down at her hand bouncing off mine, not knowing why it made me so uneasy. Then I smiled back.

Her brow creased. 'You're Nick,' she said, her eyes brightening.

'Yes.' I felt absurdly flattered and happy. 'I'm Nick.' And even if she never recognised me again, that was fine. Somewhere in that pinball-head was Lola Nan, and she knew me.

'You said you'd visit me,' she said.

'I'm sorry, Lola Nan. I've been, um . . . I haven't been well.'

'Oh.' She rocked a little in her armchair, patted my hand. Pat, pat. 'Oh dear.'

We sat in silence for a while. It was fine.

She said, 'What happened to that boy?'

'Who, Lola Nan?'

'The Boy.'

'Me, Lola Nan. That's me. I'm here.'

'No, no, no.' She clicked her tongue. 'The *Boy*. That boy who always talked to me. Fair hair. Tall. Lovely manners, so he had.'

There were spiders running up and down my vertebrae. I was watching her hand, the one that was patting mine. You know what? If my hand was invisible, it would look like she was patting a cushion of air. I curled my fingers round hers to hold them still.

'He always talked to me,' she said, nodding. 'Lovely boy. Where's he gone?'

I found my voice. 'I don't know, Lola Nan.'

'Is he coming back?' She tugged her fingers out of mine, began patting my hand again. Pat, pat. 'I wish he'd come back.' Pat, pat.

I hoped not. I pulled my hand away quite violently. 'I have to go, Lola Nan.'

Her fingers hovered, then she clenched her knobbly fist and looked at me sadly. 'He won't come back, will he?'

'No,' I said after a small hesitation. 'But I will. I'll come back and visit. I promise.'

Her eyes sparked and she smiled at me.

I closed the door of her room as softly as I could and then I got out of there, fast as I could. I wasn't much use at running yet but I tried. At least she was on the ground floor.

The big front door was too far away and I was in pain

again. The sick-yellow carpet advanced and receded before my eyes; I needed to breathe air that wasn't sodden with chemicals and cabbage and body fluids. Now. I fumbled at the fire door.

When I clanked the security bar down and shoved out into the street, sucking in great breaths of fresh air, the weather had turned. Autumn wasn't autumn any more, I thought as I stared at the lacework of stripped trees against an ice-blue sky. I'd only been in Lola Nan's overheated cell for half an hour, but winter had set in while my back was turned.

Oh fine. Yeah. It was *winter*.

And that would account for the frost in my spine.

28

It felt strange, being out in such a crowd, and I wasn't sure I liked the press of bodies, but I wasn't scared or anything. I just wasn't used to normal life. I hadn't gone far from the house in the weeks since I'd got home from hospital. I'd forgotten that people gathered in jostling hordes, laughing and swearing, sparklers fizzing and sputtering in their hands, fundraising buckets rattling hopefully. Just visible beyond the black mass of bodies was the glow of a massive hellish bonfire, throwing whirls of sparks skywards. Above us was a Hallowe'en sky, ominous clouds floodlit by a now-you-see-it-now-you-don't moon, while beneath my feet the park grass was turning to beaten mud. From the burger van drifted an overpowering fried-onion smell, nauseating and enticing all at once.

Looking round for Allie, I saw that Shuggie was with her. They were too far away to hear, but Shuggie was keeping up a stream of consciousness in her ear. Allie seemed to be ignoring him, then she rolled her eyes, shook her head, hid her grin. After a bit she laughed, then dug him in the ribs. I never knew anybody could look as smug as Shuggie did then.

The raging bonfire, the eerie glowsticks, the moonlit sky: all were abruptly eclipsed by an explosion of light. Another rocket went up, and another, filling the sky with red and green fire, and the jostling and cursing melted into oohs and aahs and applause.

My eyes stung with the awe and wonder of it. Fireworks. So ordinary, so prosaic, so once-a-year predictable. So beautiful. How did somebody think of fireworks? I bet it was somebody who nearly died.

A hand on my arm. 'Hello.'

I stopped looking at the fireworks. 'Hello, Orla.'

'I'm really sorry,' she said, as if she wanted to get it out quickly.

'What for?' I said. I was going to be cool about this. Definitely. Very cool.

Besides, I couldn't get out more than one syllable at a time.

'I never came to see you.' Withdrawing her hand she folded her arms, looked over my shoulder.

'Why did you never come?' So much for being cool. I sounded like a whipped puppy that could speak English, just.

She stayed silent for ages, staring past my shoulder. It

gave me the excuse to watch her face and feel the love that went down to my bone marrow. It was a cruel sort of love: it liked squeezing my scar, too. Ouch. Oh, so what. I'd get over it. If I watched that hard beautiful face long enough I'd get sick of it. For sure. Even the nose ring.

Not yet, though.

Orla opened her mouth once, twice. At last she got it out.

'It was kind of like Aidan. Kind of the same. And I thought you were going to die. That's why and I know it's not an excuse and I'm sorry. Right?'

'Right,' I echoed.

'Anyway, I think I'm bad for you. I make you feel bad 'cause of Aidan.'

'No, you don't.' Oops, uncool. 'Whatever.'

She tugged angrily at her platinum flick of hair. 'I mean, when you feel guilty you do such fecking stupid things, you. So it was kind of my fault.'

'Not,' I said.

The rockets had stopped exploding in the sky, the moon had sailed back into view, and now white curls of light whooshed close to the ground, squealing and whooping. Bored with the lesser spectacle, a toddler on its father's shoulders started whingeing, and the man jiggled it up and down so hard I thought it was going to fall off him. I pretended to be fascinated, because I'd changed my mind: anything was better than looking at Orla.

'See if you'd died –' she said suddenly, and clamped her

lipo together

I never got to find out, because the boring fireworks faded out and the rockets started up again, bigger and better than before. The child shut up and goggled at them.

'Allie says my brother's gone,' said Orla, folding her arms and bouncing up and down on her toes as if she was trying to keep warm. It wasn't the least bit cold.

'So she says.'

'Maybe it was because he saved Allie,' she said, 'so he had to look after her.'

'Or maybe the other way round,' I said. How fanciful. I blushed. 'Sort of.'

Another silence, punctuated by explosions of light in the air, applause, the giggling shriek of a girl. I wanted Orla to go away, and I desperately wanted her to stay.

'Did it never occur to you to wait for the police?' she barked at last.

'They wouldn't have come. Not fast enough. Even Shuggie knew that.' I chewed hard on my lip. 'Even when Shuggie got them, they didn't know where to start looking.'

'Neither did you, you eejit.'

'I did when I thought about it.' Shrugging, I said mechanically: 'Anyhow, you've got to look after yourself.'

'So why don't you let people do it?'

I blinked. 'What?'

'You. You're always looking after people.' She sounded kind of angry about it. 'Allie, Kev, Shuggie. You can't trust yourself to turn your back on them, can you? Can't trust *them*.'

'That's not fair,' I began.

'Yeah. Completely fair. What are you saying, everybody's on their own? If you really think that, Nick – and you don't – then look after yourself. Look after *yourself*. You're not a frigging superhero. You're not starring in your own movie. You couldn't have saved my brother, OK?' She rubbed her eyes with her fist. 'You couldn't look after bloody Aidan on top of everybody else, for God's sake!'

Running out of words, she blinked. I swallowed hard.

'It wasn't your fault,' she said.

'It wasn't yours.'

'Yeah, but I know it.'

'Me too,' I said. 'Seeing as you've explained it all so tenderly.'

'You big stupid delusional tosser.' Orla took hold of my face. 'I love you.'

So fireworks exploded, and the sky lit up, and the crowds applauded and whooped and stamped their feet.

And Orla Mahon kissed me.

Acknowledgements

I am hugely grateful to my terrific agent, Sarah Molloy, who believed so strongly in this book. I'm also indebted to Hilary Johnson, Julia Williams and Catherine MacPhail, for their enthusiasm and good advice.

Iain Hingston and Simon Liddiard were incredibly patient and generous with advice on court procedure and criminal law. My thanks go to them and also to Mags Neison and Ewen Riddick for medical advice; to Allan Wright, who gave me useful information about the cattle insemination business; to Dorothy Liddle, who helped with the facts of school life; to Michelle Wyllie for showing me the ropes at Aberdeen Sheriff Court; and to Andrew Evans for reading over the manuscript.

A huge thank you to Sarah Odedina at Bloomsbury, and to Isabel Ford and Helen Szirtes for patient and meticulous editing.

Writing is so much easier when you have writing buddies to encourage, give feedback, and make you laugh. Too many to name, but I owe special thanks, to Linda Gillard – she knows why – and to Maggie Craig, Elizabeth Garrett and Christine Richard.